WyldBlood Magazine

Issue 6 – December 21 / January 22

Contents

Editorial – *Mark Bilsborough*	1
Vanishing Ink – *Adam Breckenridge*	2
Blood in the Water – *Sarah Dropek*	13
Eight Bar Blues and You Ain't Goin' Home – *Wayne Faust*	20
The Great Hunt – *Timothy Friend*	29
Lost to the Dark – *Frances Koziar*	39
The First Astronomers of Carrick – *Caroline Reid*	46
The Scars You Keep – *Aeryn Rudel*	56
The Truth About Fairy Tales – *Michael Teasdale*	62
GloPop – *LG Thomson*	70
A Hundred Years of Bottled Sunshine – *Matt Webb*	75
Film, TV and books – *Mark Bilsborough*	80

Editorial

Welcome to Issue 6, which rounds out our first year of publication. We've got ten stories this time around kicking off with Adam Breckenridge's *Vanishing Ink* – because what if there was an ink that made things actually vanish – and what if that was the only thing that stood in the way of the end of everything?

Fighting oppression and finding a voice in *Blood on the Water*. Time travelling musicians in *Eight Bar Blues and you Ain't Goin' Home*. Fantasy adventure in *The Great Hunt*, Prison and survival in *Lost to the Dark*, bees in space in *The First Astronomers of Carrick*, caught by the mob in *The Scars you Keep*. Shattered dreams in *The Truth about Fairy Tales* and our appetite for self-destruction laid bare in *Glo-Pop* pack the middle. Then we end with Matt Webb's *A Hundred Years of Bottled Sunshine* – therapy or punishment? All served with vintage wine and a wry smile.

It's a varied selection, covering fantasy, science fiction and with a healthy strain of horror cropping up in a few of these stories. More than ever, our fantastic writers have tackled issues and woven tales that make us think, smile, dream and shiver. I think it's our best yet – let us know if you agree!

We're back in January, Until then, enjoy the stories.

Vanishing Ink

Adam Breckenridge

Sometimes I just want to rip the curtains open and let all the devils scratching at the glass outside gaze upon me, let their weird eyes do what they will. But most days my curiosity never goes beyond the cautious peeks I steal through the edges of the curtains, at claws and black bits of flesh that press against the glass, leaving not so much as a crack for the empty depths behind them to darken through. I do this daily, though I dread the sight of them, dread the occasions that I spot a face sneering at me, which is enough to leave me so shaken that I find myself huddling for hours in the center of the room. Their faces are a terror to behold, so vicious and empty at the same time, like a well of poisoned air.

When I was a child the claws scratching on the glass were just tree branches, so harmless by day but by night I was certain it was their intention to smash through the window and crush me in their grip. I remember running to my parent's bedroom in the night, weeping into their pajamas while they laughed away my anxieties.

"Shall I chop the trees down and pulp them into stationary for our store?" my father would ask.

But they were so beautiful by day, growing up through the concrete to surround our shop, protecting us with their shadows. I thought the wind rustling the leaves were conversations they carried on above me. I wanted to climb them so I could hear what they said and maybe talk to them myself, try to convince them to protect me at night, but their lowest branches were well beyond my reach.

The trees are long gone, as is the sidewalk around the shop that they grew from. There is nothing left but me, the demons outside who endlessly taunt me, and the shop, with its thousands of jars of ink my parents left behind.

People used to come for miles to buy the ink my parents sold, because no matter what you needed it for, ours was always the best. Our apple ink produced fuller apples than anyone else's, if one needed to repair a leaky roof our patching ink could fill in a hole that would outlast the plaster around it, for a leisurely weekend our breeze ink drew a soft wind that coupled well with the shade you could draw to lie in.

Most of these inks serve no function now, as they would need some substance outside of the bounds of the shop to be of any use. What good is ink for drawing tulips when there is no light for them, or ink for drawing locks when there is no one to keep out, or even ink for calligraphy, when there is no one to admire your penmanship?

It was with the most childish of inks that my parents managed to save us from the nothing. Vanishing ink sold for pennies a pint and once you matured past the age of seven you could only turn your nose up at any kid still naïve enough to be delighted by its trickery, though it is a wondrous thing the first time your mother draws a line on a sheet of paper for you and then inches her fingers towards it until they cross the line and disappear. Carefully she would wait just long enough for your astonishment to register before shoving her whole arm across, a clean slice across her arm precisely where the line was drawn. Then quickly, lest your amazement grow to alarm, she pulled it back to show that it's still intact.

I remember spending hours with my first well of vanishing ink, drawing a line on a sheet of paper as my mother had done and experimenting with sticking my arm across quickly and slowly, waving it back and forth, hoping to shake loose the mystery of its function. Every child, after awhile, gives in to the temptation to stick their head across the line and see what happens, and every child learns then that their head is still there, just not visible to others. This leads inevitably to the first time you draw a line of ink on the ground and jump across it, only to learn that the ink doesn't work more than a few inches above the line you drew and that when you land you will at most find yourself standing on invisible feet and that even if you keep them invisible, the effect wears off after a few minutes.

Thus every child grows weary of vanishing ink quickly after the disappointing limitations of the substance are revealed. And so I couldn't help but groan when I came downstairs into the shop to find my mother playing with it, sticking her arm across and pulling it back out.

"Mom, what are you doing?" I asked, "that stuff is for babies."

"I'm thinking about nothing," she said, and I understood what she meant.

My mother, like so many others, had been increasingly bogged down by worries over the growing patches of nothingness that were emerging around the world. It was not the first time we had had problems with nothingness. Like thunderstorms or solar flares, occasional bursts of nothingness would appear and vanish as quickly as they had come. It was treated the same way as any other disaster, with police cordoning off the patches until they faded away and warnings on the news of increased activity of nothingness. I even saw a patch of nothing once, when I was out playing with friends.

It's hard to say how big it was, since the size of a patch of nothing is difficult to determine, but it was relatively small and, like all nothing, lacking in color, which is impossible to describe unless you've seen it. We had fun throwing rocks and sticks at it, dared each other to jump in, though none of us ever would have done it, as it would have meant that we'd cease to exist.

But no one had ever seen anything like this new kind of nothing before. Not only were patches appearing and not fading away, word was the patches were growing and expanding too. Some people even spoke of entire towns being swallowed up by it, though it only seemed to happen in places far away. No one knew what to make of it.

So I understood what she meant by nothing. What I did not understand was what vanishing ink had to do with nothingness.

I gave it no more thought until a few weeks later. My mind had been too much elsewhere. The stories of the nothing were getting worse: the patches were growing bigger and getting closer, close enough that the stories weren't so easily dismissible now. People we trusted had come in to tell us they'd seen it for themselves, that this was like no nothing that had ever come before. Some were planning to flee, everyone was on edge, which is what made it so strange when I came down from my room and I saw mom and dad in the back room playing with vanishing ink again.

"Are you guys seriously still playing with that stuff?" I asked as I approached them, then reached out my arm towards the line they had drawn on the tabletop.

"Don't," my mother screamed and batted my arm away. I jumped back, my heart racing. She had never yelled at me before.

"What was that about?"

My dad spoke up.

"This isn't the usual vanishing ink son," he said, "we've made a special batch of it, like nothing anyone has made before. Watch."

He went to the refrigerator, rummaged for a minute, then came back with a carrot. Carefully he nudged the carrot point first across the line and it vanished as you would expect. When it was halfway across he stopped and pulled it back. But while I was expecting it to re-emerge fully intact, instead it was still half missing.

"Anything that vanishes across this line vanishes for good," my mom said, "it doesn't just make it look like nothing is there, there really is nothing there."

I stared at them in confusion.

"But who's gonna want to buy an ink that does that?"

They looked at each other.

"This isn't to sell, son," my dad said, "it's to protect us from the nothing."

Again, I understood what he meant. But how vanishing ink, no matter how it was modified, could help us was beyond me.

"You still haven't figured it out?" my mom asked after a moment of silence. She continued before I could answer. "The ink, if we made it right, works both ways. Not only will it turn something into nothing, it also turns nothing into something."

"But what will it turn into?" I asked.

"There's no way to know," she said, "it could literally be anything, but what's important is that it won't be nothing. Nothing is absolute, there's, well, nothing we can do to stop it, but if we can turn it into something tangible we can face it, find a way to stop it. This gives us at least a little cause for hope."

Not much, as we would find out. I thought I had finally worked up the nerve to talk about it, but I guess its still too tender for me. My parents died protecting these inks from the plagues, the riots, the fires and the hunger of the darkness and every other evil thing that came down upon us as the nothing took over. Sometimes I think the nothing might have been better.

My wells of ink for drawing food have been running dry, and there are few things more frustrating than to crave an apple only to find halfway through drawing one that you only have enough ink for a core. Retrieving more ink, woefully, meant having to descend down into the shop to face naked the eyes of the demons who gather round the windows down there as I fumbled around among the thousands of jars of ink that my parents had never bothered to label. There have been times when I starved for days rather than face them because I needed the imminent threat of death to inspire me to confront them.

This time though I had a new plan to take as much time as I needed for as many inks as I needed without having to fear their gaze. During one of my searches for ink to make food I stumbled across ink that could draw masks. I had forgotten we had it, though it had always been so popular during Halloween that my parents could barely mix it fast enough. My dad always had to draw my masks for me, because I could never handle the ink well enough myself to draw anything other than crude pseudo-faces.

At the time I couldn't see any practical use for the ink, but, because I found myself tearing up for the nostalgia it brought me, I took some back upstairs with me. I'm grateful now I did, because it gave me an inspiration. My hand is much steadier than it used to be, and I find now that I am able to draw a passable demon mask. Perhaps I could make them think I was one of them. Maybe I would even start to believe, just a little bit, that I was one of them too, and I would have less cause to fear them.

It was terrifying to step into the gaze of the demons who pressed against the window, though I tried my best to move like them, wisp-like and fluid, as though I might vanish into the shadows at any moment. I found it impossible, however, to resist breaking away from my dance and running my finger against the hilt of the sword I always carried with me when I went downstairs. It seemed my ruse was working – the demons weren't cackling as they are wont to do – there was no rattling of the glass, no scratching of claws, but some of them imitated my movements as I undulated my limbs and body across the floor, snickering to themselves.

Just as I was about to enter the storeroom, I turned to look at them one more time and saw the leering face of one of them standing inches from mine. I was so startled by its unexpected appearance that, without thinking, I unsheathed my sword and cut its laughing head off. The head splattered when it hit the floor, forming a stain of ink in the shape of its face that began to eat through the wood, leaving only the impression of its eyes, nose and mouth. Soon, where it had burned through completely, I could see the black void that was usually blocked from my view by the mass of demons. The body was draining into it, returning to the nothingness it had come from.

I ran into the storeroom and retrieved some of the ink for filling in holes. When I came back, the body was gone, though the hole in the shape of the demon's face was still there. I knew if I left it long enough the nothingness would start to seep through, transforming into more demons as it passed the demarcation of the vanishing ink.

I had already witnessed this evolution once before after my parents had safeguarded the store with the vanishing ink they had prepared for it. For weeks the bucket had sat in our kitchen as the nothingness moved closer and then became a self-evident presence when patches of it began to appear on the horizon. Many people in town tried to flee, but they came back to report that the nothingness had surrounded us. We had become a floating island just a few miles across and what space was left to us was shrinking every day. The despair was unbearable to me. I did not fear for myself – that fear I left to my parents – but to see the few people left around us, friends, neighbors, other shop owners, so crushed by the despair of the imminent destruction of every bit of life any of us had ever known, and knowing all the while that a solution that could save us all was sitting in a bucket in the kitchen, was unbearable to me.

"Do we have enough ink to save the town?" I asked my mom.

"We barely even have enough for the shop," she told me.

"How many people do you think we can fit in the shop?" I asked.

"Sweetie, this is not going to be easy to understand, but we're only going to use this ink for the three of us."

"What? Why?" I asked, but didn't give her a chance to answer before I went on, "what about my friends and their parents, what about uncle Mark and aunt Judy, what about –"

"We can't save all of them," she shouted, "we're going to be lucky if we can even manage to save ourselves."

That stopped me. In all the chaos that had surrounded us I hadn't even once doubted the certainty that they would see me through alive. I knew others were dying in other parts of the world, but I thought we would be spared; that nobody I knew would die. I think my mom realized what a weight she had dropped on me because she quickly added, "sweetie, your dad and I are going to do everything we can to get the three of us through this. Times like this require great sacrifice and hard decisions. We wish we could save everyone in the world…"

But I had stopped listening, burdened as I was in equal parts by this sudden understanding of the unstoppable destruction coming down on us and by how quickly my naivete towards it had been destroyed. I aged ten years in those few moments. When my mom stopped speaking I said, "yes, okay," not even sure if it was a coherent response, then went to my room.

For weeks afterwards, as friends came to say goodbye to us and as the life in our town descended from despair to chaos, all I could see when I looked at anyone else (including my reflection) was death. The fires that burned day and night, the noise of looters, the screams of women being raped and men begging for their lives all suited my mood to an alarming degree – what a state I had gotten myself into to be a twelve-year-old boy who took comfort in such a symphony.

My parents decided to take action and protect ourselves the first time anyone threw a rock through one of our windows. They said their plan had been to wait until the nothingness was closing in before using the vanishing ink, but the morning after the window-smashing they were outside our sidewalk with their largest quills, drawing a barrier on the ground. I thought it would make everything on the other side invisible to us but, as my dad explained, someone or something had to actually cross the line for it to work. I got my first demonstration of this when a bird almost flew into our store but vanished when it crossed the line. A few days later a few strays from a mob charging down the street tried to attack our shop. Their sudden disappearance stopped the rioters in their tracks and an eerie calm settled on the street such as we had not heard for days. I watched them from my bedroom window and saw among them so many of the faces of friends and relatives who I had wanted to save just a few days before.

I had been so isolated from the chaos of the streets that I had not realized just what kind of madness had come to grip them, but I could barely register the faces I saw out there as human. I remember thinking at the time (with no notion of the irony to come) that it was as though demons had stolen their faces and were wearing them as masks. There was no love or thought or intelligence in those eyes. There is in fact no word for what I saw except nothing.

For the first time in weeks I felt some sense of security again. The rioters left our shop alone and quickly our new state of affairs began to seem normal. My parents continued to mix ink with what supplies we still had in the shop, mostly inks for food and water. I had grown up watching them mix inks and so for awhile I gave no thought to their labors, but it started to bother me that they worked so studiously at it.

"What's the point?" I asked them one evening, "if the nothingness destroys everything except our shop, then why bother? We're just going to die anyway."

They winced at the question.

"Things aren't that hopeless, sweetie," my mom said.

"You think we haven't been planning for that, son?" my dad added, then gestured for me to come over. He had a notebook in front of him, the notebook he used to write out ink formulas. Though I hadn't quite learned how to read them yet, I understood something of their language. A formula for a simple ink, like for drawing water, required only a few words and symbols, but a more complex ink, like for brewing thunderstorms, required four or five lines to write out. I had never seen a formula longer than seven lines but the one he was working on took up the entire page, or so I thought, until he started flipping back through the notebook to show five, ten, twenty, thirty-four pages of formula.

"What kind of ink is that complicated?" I asked

"An ink like no one has ever even attempted before," he said, "it's an ink that will let us draw a new world. With one jar we can create an entire new earth from scratch. It'll be a great opportunity to build a perfect world, or at least a better one than this, one where there is no nothingness, where everything will be beautiful."

"But how will we populate it?"

"I don't know. We might have to take solace in filling it with plants and insects and leave the course of evolution to take over again, but maybe we'll be able to mix an ink that will let us draw people into existence."

"If the ink works," I said.

"Yes," my dad sighed, "if the ink works."

I don't know why that demon alone attempted to enter, but it has been a long time since any of them tried to get in here. Most of them can't get past the line my parents drew, but I've never understood why. I suspect that, even with their wicked smiles, they fear the something as much as I fear the nothing. It requires only the one though, who sneaks past unnoticed and comes to my bed as I sleep, to put an end to me and what little of the world I have left to myself.

I still had the ink, but when my parents died they took with them the secret of how to make them and how to tell them apart. So familiar were they with each of their inks that they never labeled the jars they came in, discerning instead from the thousands of inks by scent, pouring out the customer's requests by their nose. The smells have no logic to them. An ink with the scent of lemons produced a length of rope, but the smell of sulfur drew a bouquet of roses. Eventually, through trial and error, I catalogued what inks did what, and now I do what I can to manage my dwindling supplies.

But there is one ink in particular I search for, one among the thousands of inks that just may be my salvation. I remember the weeks my parents spent brewing it. I had never seen them put so much work into a batch of ink, mixing ingredients I'd never seen them use before. Eventually they produced a jar that looked no different from any other but whose scent was never the same no matter how many times I smelled it.

"This is the accomplishment of a lifetime son," my dad said, "an ink that can draw new worlds. No one's ever made it before, we're the first ones to ever do it."

And then they died before they could ever use it or remind me which among the thousands of jars it was. I'm alone now, with no hope except to find the ink, one among the thousands of jars under the watchful eyes of the demons.

A demon found its way into my room. I screamed when I awoke and saw it hunched over on top of my desk. It was a fraction of the size of the one I encountered the other day, tinier, in fact, than any other I had seen in glimpses out the window. It made no response to my cry, nor any reaction when I sprung forward with the knife I kept under my pillow for a purpose such as this. I stopped short just as I was about to bring the blade down on its neck. It was using my nature inks to draw a meadow on the desktop.

I set down my knife and put my hand into the meadow. It had been so long since I had felt wind that even the breath of it on my palm was enough to awaken so many buried childhood memories – times happier than any I had known in a long time. I had sworn to myself that I would never forget what it was like to lie down in the grass, but it seemed such joys had escaped me after all.

My hand made the demon aware of my presence for the first time and it looked up at me. I didn't fear its eyes as I did those of the others. It showed a gentleness I had never witnessed in them before. Was this perhaps not a demon at all but some other creature so alike in outward appearance as to be inevitably mistaken for one?

As I was lost in thought it wrapped a tiny hand around one of my fingers so suddenly that I scarcely had time to react. I yelped at the touch before realizing how humane it was, its skin rough and cold, as it had probably just come from outside. It looked at me, then drew its eyes towards the meadow.

"Perhaps you should devour it as you have all the rest of this world," I said and snatched my hand away from it.

I spent the next many hours on my bed staring at the creature, wanting to trust it but afraid that if my eyes strayed from it it would use that moment to pounce and put an end to me. But it never did any more or less than stare at its meadow and occasionally poke at it to flesh out the trees or float a couple of clouds above the scene. Finally I came over and ran my finger along one of the tiny blades of grass and found I could stretch it out much as if I were sketching. The demon was staring intently at my work. I pinched the blade with both hands and molded it, making it resemble a leaf. I tried turning it into a tree, but the material was stretching too thin for that kind of manipulation, so instead I curled the leaf up, then knocked it over and fashioned it into a log, with mold growing on the topside. When I finished, the demon reached out and caressed my design, showing the kind of fascination I would expect from an infant.

Then I had an idea.

Delicately I picked up the demon, cringing at its texture on my skin. I carried it downstairs, holding it in front of me like a shield. The demons were gathered as usual around the shop windows, pressing their faces against them, more faces than ever it seemed, watching with intent at this new spectacle that paraded before them. The demon in my hand had not proven as much of a protection against the violence of their glares as I had hoped, but this was not why I had brought it down with me. Rather I was taking the profound risk of taking it to the storeroom, because I had an idea of just which ink it might lead me to.

When the demon saw the buckets lined on their shelves, it leapt from my hand and crashed against them, scattering ink in every direction. I panicked as I watched it toss my food inks against the wall, droplets transforming into tiny globules of bread, vegetables and pies as they spilled out. I lunged for it as it sent a bucket flying into the opposite wall, which then exploded into a display of fireworks, singeing my hair and burning holes in my clothes. Another bucket burst into bouquets of flowers, an avalanche of rope fell and entangled me, I slipped on the contents of another bucket that had marbles spilling out from it. And, just when I was about to grab it, it latched onto a jar on a shelf just above my head. I reached up and took it down with the demon still clinging to it. Unlike the other inks, this one was a swirl of colors that never stopped moving. How many times had my hands passed by this jar without noticing it before? My anger at the demon was forgotten as I dipped a finger in and drew a circle on the wall. I filled it in, then scooped the circle out of the wall and molded it into a sphere. It took on the appearance of a tiny planet. I had another idea. I picked up the planet, then stepped out into the main room and hurled it against the glass. For once it was the demons feared me as it splattered against the glass. They cleared away from where it hit and I caught a rare glimpse of the emptiness behind them from which the demons materialized.

"Perhaps you're not such a bad fiend after all," I said, picking up the jar it still clung to and taking all of us back upstairs.

I don't think I fear the demons anymore. I slept better last night than I have since before the branches of the trees started calling for me against the windowpanes.

I took the bold inspiration this morning to tear open the curtains on my bedroom window. There was no sign of the demons who usually perched out there. I can't recall my bedroom view ever being fully exposed to the abyss before and there is something so horrifying, yet beautiful, about the sight of the expansive vacuum. I found it strangely inspiring to sit before it and experiment with the ink.

It was like no ink I had ever used before. My first thought was to draw a meadow with it, as the demon had, but each stroke of the pen had a way of taking on a life of its own so that my attempt to draw a blade of grass somehow resulted in a stick figure who danced about the desk before jumping to the floor and running through a crack in the wall. I would try instead to let my hand do as it wished but the results were too random to be of any use. The only consistency I noted was that the outcome of my pen was always organic, and in testing this I attempted to draw a car and wound up instead with a jackal who was lively enough to try to bite my finger.

All the while the demon watched my efforts intently, never blinking as its eyes followed the movements of my hand. Its unyielding gaze began to wear on me, so to temper my annoyance I took my pen and swiped it across its cheek. To my astonishment the ink lightened its skin tone from black to brown. The demon looked up at me. Its expression was unreadable. I swiped my pen across its right eye and it turned from solid white to a deep, human brown. I followed suite with the other eye but found the sight of its human gaze staring out from that demon body to be, in a way, even more disturbing than the glare of one of the demons outside.

"What are you?" I asked, but it only stared at me.

I dipped my pen in the ink again and swiped it across the black slash of its mouth, which turned it into full, red lips. They tried to speak, but must have lost the trick to it, because all they could do was flap open and closed without making any sound. I turned the black scar of its nose into a fuller, plumper form. A thing of beauty, I thought, there is something divine beneath this crust, something, if not human, then cloaked in the beauty of humanity. I found myself becoming aroused by it, though I had no idea if what I uncovered was male or female. The world was devoured before I had a chance to find out if I was gay or not, and so I found the strokes of my pen quickened by the imminence of this discovery.

Its form was too tiny – I had to broaden my strokes to stretch its body out. With a vast sweep of my wrist I gave it arms that could embrace me. Its body took the form of a woman, with full, dark breasts; her skin was so much darker than mine, and smoother. I had never seen a naked woman before and here she was taking shape before my eyes, her body doing more of the work than my pen, guiding my lines through her movements.

I couldn't tell her ethnicity, and it could very well have been that she didn't have one. "Are you a real woman?" I asked her. She shrugged. I was unsure what to make of this. "Do you understand what I'm saying?" I asked. She smiled at me. There were still bits and pieces of the blackened flesh of a demon clinging to her skin and I spun her around to try to fill in whatever spots my pen had missed. I had a notion that perhaps completing her would grant her the power of speech, but the words never came, nor did her hair, for nothing grew on her scalp. Yet she was beautiful – more beautiful than I ever could have imagined.

"Where do you come from?" I asked. She pointed out the window, at a spot in the void. "Do you mean just from out there?" I asked and swept my arm in an arc. She shook her head no and pointed at the same spot. "What's out there?" I asked, but she only smiled.

I approached the window without fear, I think, for the first time in my life. I focused my eyes on the spot she had indicated, but no matter how much I wanted to imagine a lone light in the brightness, I could see nothing there.

"Are there other places like this?" I asked without turning away from my study of the emptiness, "other spots that survived?" Then I jumped as I felt something touch my back, then realized it was her hand. Before I could turn to her she wrapped her arms around my waist and I could feel her standing on tiptoes to rest her chin on my shoulder. I was startled by the tranquility I felt from her embrace. It had been so long since I had felt any kind of human contact. I twisted around in her arms to face her. Her eyes sparkled.

"I want to know everything there is to know about you."

I held my pen up to her face. She took it and, stepping away from me, began to draw.

I watched as she transformed my room into a likeness of the meadow I had first seen her create. She had a mastery of the ink that I couldn't fathom: she could flick her wrist and raise a crop of grass and, with an identical flick, spring forth a sunflower. With a few more twists and flourishes she populated it with an ark of mice, birds, raccoons and whatever other creatures she felt inspired to bring forth.

When she finished, she turned and stared at me, her chin thrust out just a touch.

"You haven't answered my question," I said, but she only thrust her chin out more. There was something enticing in her stance, not just that she was naked, but that she seemed to be teasing me. Perhaps it was because she was so newly formed that I did not expect such sass from her.

I took a step towards her and she drew a fence between us. As I stepped over it she flicked the pen and raised it several more feet off the ground. The shot to my groin sent me toppling. Through the gagging pain I heard a sound that stopped my breath. Laughter. Her laughter. I stood up as best as I could manage.

"I want to hear your voice," I said, "you must speak beautifully."

She turned and beckoned me to follow her down the stairs, all the while dashing out casual creations with the pen. A quick swipe and a waterfall ran down the wall. Another flick and fish jumped from the stream below it. She glanced behind occasionally to smile as I followed her down the stairs. With a flick of the pen she drew a miniature sun that lit up the room as I had not seen it lit since customers regularly came through the doors. It was more than just the brightness (brighter than anything I had seen in years) that was painful, the illumination brought back more happy memories than I cared for. Every lighted corner recalled joyous old days – the time I stood outside that window over there and pretended to be a ghost watching the comings and goings of the store, a fantasy ruined by my mother and father constantly waving to me and pointing me out to smiling customers; the first jar of ink I ever sold, to an old lady who tipped me a quarter for being such a fine salesman; my mother pausing from organizing the shelves to watch the sun set through the front door.

I thought she was heading to the storeroom, but she only turned to it long enough to draw a veil of ivy to cover the entrance. She moved with divine randomness, drawing as it pleased her and by no logic that I could discern. I found myself growing bored of her creations and focusing instead on her figure. I never thought I would get a chance to know the touch of a woman and now that one of such godly beauty stood before me, turning the store I had lived in my entire life into a biosphere, I could think only of how badly I wanted her. She seemed to sense my thoughts, because she turned to me and gave an inviting smile.

"Can you tell me what I'm thinking right now?" I asked her, but she merely smiled again and beckoned me to follow her.

I would have followed her past the line that divided the store from the nothingness outside, or so I thought, until I saw that was where she was actually heading.

She forced open the front door, which whined on its hinges from the many years it had remained shut. The coldness of the vacuum outside chilled me even from a distance, yet she seemed not the least bit bothered by it. An edge of the sidewalk still remained, stopping where my parents had drawn the vanishing line so many years before. Not a demon was in sight. She stepped up to the rim, placed the nib of the pen at the edge, and drew an arc about six feet high. I say she drew, but the pen left no record of its passage, yet she seemed satisfied with her work. I stood several feet away and when she saw that I had not approached, she came to me, grabbed me by the hand, and marched me to the barrier. Standing so close to the nothingness was more terrifying than the manifestations of the demons, but she showed no fear. Instead, she stepped through her invisible doorway, vanishing as she crossed the line.

There had been no hesitation in her step, she had crossed as casually as if she were going into the next room. I stood stunned and alone, unwilling to follow though it was clearly what she wanted me to do. I recalled the words of my father, saying if I ever crossed the line the abyss would swallow me, but there was no place she could have come from except from the other side of it. I could feel her eyes on me. She was beckoning me, and I came to understand as I hesitated that even if I crossed to my death there was nothing waiting for me in the shop or my room. I wanted to be free from my memories, free from the walls, free to create new worlds with the Eve I had helped shape into being and who now held the promise of a different kind of future, one that was composed of something rather than nothing.

I could sense her laughter. I stretched my hand across the barrier. There was a peculiar lack of sensation interrupted by a faint tingling of warmth. I could feel her presence, feel her taking my hand. She was the only thing I had any faith in. I stepped across.

Adam Breckenridge is an Overseas Traveling Faculty member for the University of Maryland Global Campus, and travels world teaching American military stationed overseas. He's currently based in South Korea. He has eighteen short story publications and his fiction has most recently appeared in Clockwork, Curses and Coal from World Weaver Press, Mystery Weekly and Horror Addicts Press.

Blood in the Water

Sarah Dropek

The Men never used our names. They simply called us The Daughters, singled us out only by our numbered talismans they said helped keep us safe from the blood hunters.

And while we were made to memorize their names and their Fathers' before them and back and back, they did not know that I was Katerin. And it was the first reason I hated them.

I didn't mind the ten of us girls and Mother being made to sleep in a large tent far away from their camp. I didn't even mind their suspicious eyes sliding over us as we grew and played with the boys outside. But knowing when I prayed at their feet that they saw me and only thought, Eleven, sparked a fire in my belly no water could extinguish.

One day, as if on the whim of the wind, the Men instructed us we could no longer be near the boys. We had been celebrating Mei's ninth birthday that morning with them and had come home crying to Mother that evening about how Father Burgess had broken up the party to take the boys back.

"To the safe side of camp," he'd said.

I can still remember Mother's strange grin as she consoled our whimpering in the tent that night, her lips spread too wide and too red against her teeth shining in the candlelight.

"You're going to be women soon," she had cooed over our hushed sniffles.

"Why does that mean we can't see the boys?" Mei cried. She'd been admiring Travis from afar and I knew she had hoped he would give her a kiss on her birthday. Now she might never be any closer to him than the large swath of forest the Men kept between our camps.

"I can see I was too kind in waiting so long," Mother muttered to herself. Then louder, she looked to all of us with solemn eyes and repeated the story of our ancestors we'd been taught since birth.

"When the blood hunters came crumbling from the deserts that had spread over the earth like fire, they came for us out of desperate thirst. It took us too long to realize that they could smell our blood in the air through every nick, cut, or scratch. We ran and hid and fought and died until barely any of us were left, until your Grandfather Maren found this forest and found the precious river in it protected him. In water, the scent of blood did not travel. And so, we made our place here."

"Grandfather Maren saved us," Mother said, folding her hands across her chest as we did every evening. "It is in his honor we pray at the feet of the Men who continue to keep us safe. We've never had ten young girls at once. For years we have let you play with the boys because there was no harm in it so long as you were careful not to play too rough. And you all have been so careful. But you will bleed soon, and we must protect the Men. That is why you cannot play together any longer."

"Bleed?" I asked, and Mother frowned at me. She was always frowning at me because I talked more than I listened, and I pestered her about the point of praying to a Grandfather I had never known.

But the other girls wanted to know, too. So she sighed and told us about our bodies and how they made us dangerous but necessary. She told us about the triangular talismans we have all had from birth, passed down from our mothers when they died to keep us safe until we could serve the community as they had. Everyone's eyes darted to the pieces of wood we were told to keep hidden. Mei, Number One, looked back and forth from her talisman to mine.

"Katerin," she whispered so Mother couldn't hear. "yours is so...new."

Blood rushed to my face and my cheeks burned in dismay. My hands passed over the rough edges and sharp corners of my talisman that looked nothing like the smooth oil-worn, deep brown of Mei's.

Later in the night, while the other girls slept, I asked Mother about it. She told me I was her second child, that she was my Blood Mother. Her lips curled in a satisfied smile as she turned my talisman over in her palm, a raw mirror to her own, where the etched number six had been worn down in the center to shallower valleys from her thumb's constant path over it.

"I am blessed I stopped my monthly bleeding after you were born. They let us both live," she murmured, as if the Men might still change their minds if it was spoken aloud.

By the flickering flame of a lone candle, I searched her face. But the sharp curve of her chin and the dainty tip of her nose seemed nothing like my broad features. I wondered if she was telling the truth, then remembered it was a sin to question Mother and Men. Sensing my turmoil, she returned the talisman safely to my pocket.

Her eyes stared hard at me as she said mine was the first new talisman needed in generations, and I should not waste its gift with any more of my doubt and questions. I went to sleep that night clutching the simple triangle my Mother had turned from an object of comfort into a weapon she wielded against me.

It is six more years of watching my sisters get pregnant and give birth in the river before I understand how Mother hates me. Six years of seeing my sisters have boys and live, or birth girls and drown at my Mother's hands. But I do not become pregnant, no matter the matches Mother makes for me. And my monthly cycle bled into the safety of the river's water, sometimes with sisters, but often alone, is my punishment.

When we bleed, we are only allowed back to camp after a week of wading in the water to hide from the demons. Our skin is so soaked through that it sloughs off, gathering under our fingernails that itch at it for days after we emerge. We are red and raw on the outside but emptied of our threat.

It is hard for me to kneel at the feet of the Men when I return. But Mother reminds me, is always reminding me, if I had fought blood hunters as our ancestors did before Grandfather Maren and watched the tongues and teeth of them suck a person dry while they still lived, I would welcome the water. She says my knees would bend for the Men without pain or force to pray if I had seen my own brother die when Crea lost her baby in the night and brought death upon us. When I tell her if I had stopped to see, it would mean I'd have died with him, she says nothing.

The rain starts softly in the early morning when the world within our tent still appears only in shades of grey. Beside me, Mei clutches at a child she hopes grows inside her as she sleeps. She is my only sister left from the original ten of us and though she disapproves of how I agitate Mother, I know she stays close for the same reason as me. The ghosts of our sisters that hide in their daughters' faces around us is too much to bear alone.

I push up onto my elbows and peer over my belly at Mother's cot by the entrance. A snore drags from her throat and the fog that surrounds her head from hot air meeting cold obscures her for a moment. I indulge myself in a sleepy fantasy that she truly doesn't exist anymore. I wonder at all of the ways life could be different.

Without Mother watching, warning, and punishing me, I could try to convince Mei and the younger girls to rise against the Men who kill us in the name of protecting us. We could escape the forest together and discover places evil might not roam the earth, sniffing out our blood. We could be free.

But the fog clears around her in a chilled wind that pushes into the tent from the storm growing outside and I know, even without her, nothing would change. The Men would still breed us and keep us penned away from them like animals. They can see no other way to live than to control us. Mother just makes it so they don't have to dirty their hands killing us themselves.

She was ready to kill me, too, offered it, even. The Eleventh woman. One too many to feed if I couldn't perform my duties. But the Men let me have one more chance and Mathew was a productive match. When I finally became pregnant, Mother took to sleeping by the soft flap of the tent with her bag packed underneath her. She doesn't trust me or my womb. A fear that has flung her more fervently towards faith. If she could sleep at the feet of the Men she worships, I know she would. But she is made to stay away with the rest of us as our Guardian.

The rain falls heavier on the tent and a knowing dread tightens my chest. I am the farthest along out of all of us. Just yesterday, Mother told Father Crawley to ready the men for moving camp after the birth. The storm will offer extra protection from blood hunters catching the scent.

Whether my body is ready or not, I will walk with her today to the river. She will give me teas and tonics to stir the child to birth. I will leave with a baby boy or I will not leave at all.

Mother was older when she had me and made herself useful to the Men after my birth, caring for all the other motherless baby girls, nursing them with her prolific milk. They waited to see if her bleeding would stop. But I am only nineteen. I will not be afforded the same compassion.

I step quietly around the other girls in the tent so as not to wake them. Either pregnant or young, the move will be hard on them today and they need whatever rest they can get. I look at Mei's eyes closed in a calm crescent moon and dare to hope she will miss me when she holds my daughter after I am gone.

I flex my fingers in the cold morning, urging my blood to reach and warm them as I pack my meager possessions. The last item I can claim as mine in a life that is barely my own at all is the talisman. I run my fingers over the still sharp corners of the triangle in its crude impersonation of a womb. It will be the only evidence to my daughter I ever existed after Mother drowns me.

I picture my baby as a bumbling toddler, innocently slicing herself on the talisman's edge, as any child might. Blood drips down her plump, pale skin. In the darkness behind her, I see no evil, simply my Mother's sickening smile. I shiver at the image and realize I'm pressing my thumb harder than I should dare against the corner of the wood.

When I pull away, the two lines of my talisman look up at me from my hand, slitted eyes, staring, waiting to devour me and the daughter that will come after me in a long line of dead women. And there's a part of me that welcomes it now, death as a freedom from this captivity.

I used to dream of taking Mei and the rest of my sisters with me to escape the forest and the Men, now I only dream of escaping it myself, even if death is the only way out.

I hear Mother snort awake behind me and I cinch my bag closed, placing it under Mei's cot for her to dole out to the girls after I'm gone.

"Do you feel ready?" Mother asks, closing the tent after looking out at the storm that will make our walk to the river slippery with mud.

The child inside me stirs at her voice as if already knowing I won't be the one around to mother it.

"Ready to have a baby or to die?" I spit back, emboldened by the forces in motion I cannot control to give words to my anger more than I ever have.

"Katerin! You must not test me like this. Every time I hope it's the last time I will hear your blasphemy and that you will stop, but this is it. The men will pray over you today for a boy, from kindness, reverence even, for how you grow our community of survivors. Do not tempt them to be insincere in their words with your own weakness of faith," she threatens.

I laugh in one sharp spurt, "your faith truly is blind if you think they have any care for us at all. The only reason they wish for a boy is because it takes longer than they'd like to raise another girl to be their incubator."

A flare of disgust colors her cheeks as she moves closer. Her hands press to my stomach, to the daughter I know is inside me. A child Mother will love more than me because she will be made to worship the Men as Mother does, without question.

I can already see in the glint in her eyes, as she feels for the position of the child, that she is thinking about how she will raise her better than me. Dreaming about how the baby will be everything I am not.

"I'm glad you've packed," she says, stepping back. "The baby is down, and the rain will make good cover. We'll leave once I tell the girls to ready their things for the move."

Her eyes rest on where I still hold my talisman. She opens her hand for it. Safekeeping until the baby is born. Tradition.

She is halfway out of the tent with it before she turns, her eyes pinched in an expression I can't read, "Do not do anything foolish, Katerin," she says, her fingers loosely holding the talisman before she pockets it. "Get started moving around to wake the babe."

#

My child is obedient like I have been for too long. She knows what is expected of her and I am already breathing hard through sharp pains when we reach the Men, drenched from the rain.

I see anger in their eyes as I kneel before them for prayers, fighting to stay still and silent while every muscle in me aches to crouch, to move, to ease the scraping fire inside me.

They think Mother has waited too long to bring me here. They worry I'll bring the blood hunters upon us all. And for a moment I hold my breath and bear down, relishing the thought of killing everyone and being done with it. But my muscles seize up at my attempt to rush things, and I clench Mother's hand that steadies me at the feet of the Men.

Mathew sits across from me in his place as the Father. His hand barely touching mine while he prays. I look up and see the same hesitant fear he had when we were last close enough to touch. I foolishly hoped then, too, if he was different from the other men. There was something about the way his hair licked in soft curls at the back of his ears that made him seem more innocent than the rest of them. More kind. But he makes no moves to follow Mother as she leads me and the rest of the girls to the river when the praying is done.

Through the fog of pain and fear, I hate him for being a coward.

Rain runs off the tip of my nose as I try to focus only on walking, only on the sound of the damp leaves beneath our steps to the river. But I cannot rid myself of the anger, and I know Mother hears it in my panicked breaths.

"I'm sure he wants it to be a boy," she says, quiet enough that none of the others will hear behind us. Her voice is almost gentle.

For a moment I want to believe that she wishes I'll live, that she will not have to drown her own child. But then another pain roars through me and I see only excitement dance in her eyes.

"Do you really think they don't look at you and hate that you're still alive?" I hiss, unable to keep the shake out of my voice.

The ugly sound of her laughter makes my teeth clench.

"I don't bleed anymore," she chirps. "And the Men respect that I lead the girls, keep track of your cycles so they don't have to. They need me."

"Then why do you still sleep with the women?" I snarl.

The trees get thicker as we close in on the river and I grasp at their branches and trunks instead of Mother's hand.

Her silence stretches between us. When I glance at her, I'm surprised to see doubt, instead of rage, pulling at her eyebrows.

She has never wondered why the Men do not protect her on their side of camp. For a moment, I marvel at the thin crack of light showing through her armor of belief.

In my shock, I stumble on a root and it's Mei who catches me from behind. She squeezes my hand with a worried smile. I squeeze back and tears prick my eyes imagining her beautiful, round face held under water by Mother. I cannot let it continue. I will not let Mei die, even if she's been made to think death would be her purpose fulfilled.

Mother is still quiet when she helps me out of my underclothes and steps with me into the cold water. Our feet sink down and find uneasy purchase in the muddy bottom and I let her hold me up as she has held others before me. The other girls watch silently, fear and envy swirling in their eyes. Just as another wave of pain rolls through me, I glimpse young Ginnifer clutch Mei's leg. Ginnifer who will die if I do nothing.

I plead, with all of the strength I can spare, praying there is a shred of love left in her heart.

"Mama," I rasp, fighting the words out through labor that now seeps red into the river, "the Men forget our blood that puts them in danger gives them life. They forget because to them we are animals, numbered, disposable. Do not let them convince you I have to die. Love me more than the comfort they have deigned to give you."

"Katerin--"

My growl cuts her off. I grip her so tightly I worry her arms bleed from my nails, but I know she would never let it happen. The strain sinks me deeper into the river so I swallow water as I try to speak.

"No. Listen," I command, feeling with every wave of agony, I am losing time to convince her. "Girl or boy, if we leave together, we have time. I can nurse. Like you. I won't bleed. Please."

"Last time," she whispers, and I think I've convinced her to come with me. That it's like before when I used to get in trouble for not praying, not kneeling, and she always said it was the last time she'd let me do it without telling the Men, even if it never was. But then my mind is drawn back into every part of me that hurts, and I cannot breathe or think until I see her hoisting the baby out of the water.

She smiles. She coos to my crying child and walks to the bank away from me. I dip my head under the water and understand. It was not the last time she would let me get away with my insolence and pleading. It was simply the last time she needed me to heed her. The last time she needed me to be useful to her, to them.

When I surface, I watch her softly speak to my child, gently washing arms and legs at the water's edge. I reach for a fallen tree and pull myself closer, careful to keep my hips below water.

"I'll get you cleaned and to camp, handsome," she says, paying me no mind. "You'll get big and strong. You'll be beautiful. Your Daddy will teach you how to keep us safe and I'll get to look at you every time I pray at your feet. Sweet, sweet boy, you will make us stronger."

I realize then that I do not care if I'm alive if it means letting my baby turn into one of them. Not Mathew with his cowardice hidden by kind eyes, and not Mother with her evil shrouded behind belief.

"Let me hold him," I demand.

"Careful," she says as she places him in my arms and I bite my tongue.

"I only want to see him before you go."

"You'll hold him plenty when you've healed," she trills, her words edged in a darkness meant only for me to hear.

I trace tender lines down his slippery skin and wonder if love is supposed to feel so much like terror.

"He's beautiful," I whisper, brushing the improbable curls of his hair. "Perfect."

"All of our Men are," Mother says, simmering rage in her eyes as she watches me reach to deliver my child into Mei's waiting arms instead of hers.

"You're lucky beyond what you deserve, Katerin," she sneers. "I will forget the blasphemy you have spoken this very last time if you take the rest of your bleeding days here to think about how you will demonstrate your faith when you come back to camp. I will not let you poison that child with your ideas that would put his life and everyone else's at risk."

When I pull Mother underwater and hold her there, I hear the girls' screams, but I see no surprise on Mother's face. Only a desperate anger. She truly thinks I will kill her the same way she would have killed me. But I want something more for her. In the midst of her struggle, I reach into the water and fish my talisman from her pocket. Keeping a hold of her wrist, I finally let her come up for air.

She chokes and sputters and screams and doesn't realize until it's too late that I am using the sharp edges of the triangle to rip the flesh of her arms. Her blood taints the water pink again.

She stills in shocked silence, gaping at her wounds. I watch only for a moment as every piece of power she ever thought she had disappears into the river with her blood. It is the moment when she realizes she is one of us again, that she never stopped being one of us.

And then I leave the water, scooping my son from Mei's arms, counting the seconds until the blood hunters come.

Some of the girls begin to cry, whimpering questions into the air, and I hear Mei's steady voice reassure them as it has always soothed me. I take my underclothes from little Ginnifer's shaking hands and press them against my thigh to wring the rain from them. Then I reach under my skirt and use the cloth to soak up as much of my blood as I can.

"No," Mother yelps, my plan becoming clear to her as I hang the cloth from a tree limb.

It is a bright red flag beckoning the demons to her, forcing her to flee the river or die in it. Evil cannot smell blood in the water, but once they arrive, they hunt the area until they are sated. A lesson Mother used to reprimand me with when I misbehaved.

"Run back to camp," I yell to her over the rumble of thunder. "See if the Men protect you now. See if they ever really cared how much you prayed and groveled, or if they only tolerated you because you did their bidding without question. Go to them. Beg. You will finally see they are more evil than the demons they have taught you to fear."

I turn to Mei and try to look stronger than I feel.

"We'll survive together, in our own way," I say. She nods through her panicked breaths and gathers the girls together.

Mother screams after us as we begin to run, but the rain drowns most of it out and her words don't settle long enough to stick. I am glad it is the last time I will have to hear her.

I run as long as my body will let me. Mei and the girls stay behind me even though I know they could run faster to safety. When I slow down at the edge of the forest we have never been allowed to leave, the girls stop further back, afraid of the open sky beyond its edge.

"Where are we going?" Mei asks as she catches her breath beside me.

"Somewhere we can _live,_" I promise. I don't say for how long and she doesn't ask. But I look at the determined set of her brow and know however long we survive, it will be enough to be free.

I hesitate before I take another step, listening for the scramble of evil coming for us. There is nothing but the sounds of the storm and my wildly beating heart. Shielding my son from the downpour with his head tucked under my chin, I step out from the trees into the rain, wondering if the demons were ever real at all or if they had been us all along.

Sarah Dropek *writes poetry and fiction in Texas. Her work has appeared in* Herstry, Solana, *and* Mic. *You can find her sporadically on twitter @Dropek.*

Eight Bar Blues and You Ain't Goin' Home

Wayne Faust

I'd been working in Chicago for over twenty years, reviewing nearly every two-bit act that came down the pike. So that makes it all the more remarkable that on the night when I first saw Jake Wilson perform, he blew me away.

It was an icy cold night in February, a hawk wind blowing in off Lake Michigan, and needles of snow swirling in the air. I was heading for the Shady Gator, a new place on Rush Street, nestled in among the trendy dance clubs and holo-performance venues that are so popular these days. I cursed my luck in having to leave my hi-rise to check out a new act on a night like this, but it was live music, so I went. There aren't a lot of live acts out there these days, but I happen to like them. Call me old-fashioned.

As I walked into the Shady Gator, it turned out to be a lot more old-fashioned than even I would have preferred. There was no enviro program, no holographic wallscreens, just plaster walls with the brick underneath showing through in patches. Imitation cigarette smoke seeped down from tiny holes in the ceiling. Rows of thrift shop, folding chairs faced the stage. It looked like a room that had been thrown together at the last minute for a poker game. Knowing what they charge for rent on Rush Street these days, I didn't believe it for a second. But the room was warm, so I took off my coat and sat down. I counted twenty people in the audience in a space that held a couple hundred.

Jake Wilson was already into his act. The stage was tiny, barely big enough to accommodate him, and looked like it was made out of plywood. He was sitting on a stool and playing a hollow-body Martin guitar, tapping his boot in time with the music. He worked a metal slide up and down the frets, making it sound like grown men crying. He was singing through a microphone that looked like it could have been around a hundred years ago, back in the early days of radio.

Sweat dripped down Jake's black-as-pitch face, sending little beads into the air as he swayed his head back and forth. A cigarette that almost looked like the real thing hung down from one corner of his mouth. A single blue light hung from a cord above his head.

He was playing the eight bar blues. I've always loved the blues, and in spite of the obvious gimmickry of the place, Jake's music was the real deal.

You got me runnin'
You got me hidin'
You got me run hide run hide any way you want
Yeah yeah yeah

What was it about that music? There was a slow, easy groove to it that took me to another place. Instead of February in Chicago, it was suddenly a summer night on the Mississippi delta with the air dripping; I was sipping lemonade and Jack Daniel's on somebody's front porch with my feet up, listening to a freight train dwindle in the distance. I felt like I had hitched a ride on a time machine, something only a very privileged few have ever done.

A deep sadness nibbled away at the edge of my consciousness. It's not okay to be sad these days. What's there to be sad about? Nobody's hungry. Everybody's got a nice place to live. We've got a billion kinds of entertainment at our fingertips. And pills for every possible situation. But still...

Some of the old recordings I've got at home make me feel a little bit like that, at three in the morning with the music coming out of the wall. Like most music critics, I'm a better listener than a player. But back in the day, given the right combination of pills, I would drag my old Gibson out of the closet and play a little myself - until my neighbor once pushed a handwritten note beneath my door. All it said was, "Please stop singing." I never did it again.

So I write. Tribune Universal is the fifth largest communication market in the world. I get wined and dined. People respect me. I'm supposed to be an impassionate observer. But here I was, riveted to my chair by Jake Wilson.

I laid down last night
Tried to take my rest
My mind got to ramblin'
Like wild geese from the west

For a panicky moment, I felt something well up inside and I thought I was going to cry. How would I explain *that*? But then I settled down, and the music soothed me like my Mama used to do.

At the end of the show, Jake stood up and took a hesitant bow. I clapped as long and hard as I could, hoping to coax an encore out of him, but the house lights came on. The crowd filed up the stairs. No one thought to stay around and shake Jake's hand or get an autograph. People are jaded these days.

But I waited. I sat alone in my chair and tried to hang onto the feeling the music had given me. A soft hiss came from the ceiling as vacuums sucked up the ersatz smoke.

Jake Wilson left the stage and brushed by me, looking straight ahead. He smelled like sweat and something else, a dusky, clinging odor that could have been what real cigarettes had smelled like in the old days.

I ambled over to Jake, who leaned on the bar with his hand wrapped around an antique bottle of Schlitz beer. They had thought of everything.

I cleared my throat. "Excuse me," I said. "I was wondering if I could talk to you for a moment."

"Ain't got no moment," he answered, looking away. His speaking voice was as raspy as his singing voice had been.

I touched the man's sweaty arm, more to reassure myself that he wasn't a hologram than for any other reason. His skin felt hot and slick. "Please," I said, "I just want to ask you a few questions."

Jake turned towards me. His eyes were bloodshot and there were traces of yellow on his teeth.

"Ain't nobody say please much around here," he said.

"Well, I would just like to talk with you a few minutes. I've never heard anything quite like I heard tonight, at least not live anyway."

"Oh, so you a fan," he said. "Barman will get you a picture."

"I don't want a picture - I mean, a picture would be fine, but what I really want is to ask a couple questions."

His eyes darted. "You a cop?"

"Of course not. I'm a music critic. But right now I'm not thinking about that."

Jake looked up at the ceiling. "Go ahead," he said.

"How do you do that? Nobody sings the blues like that anymore. Nobody *has* the blues. Why should they?"

"That what you think? Nobody got the blues here? They got 'em all right. It be in their eyes. They got empty spots, way inside. The music reach in there and fill 'em up. Better than any o' them pills."

The man was right about that. I'd felt it myself. "And what about you?" I asked. "What does it do for you?"

Jake Wilson took a long, slow sip of beer. "I just play," he mumbled. "That's all."

Someone tapped my shoulder. I turned to see a skinny little man glaring at me. His silver hair was flawless and he wore a suit that must have cost a few thousand credits. His tie had blue music notes on a black background and it was held in place by a diamond pin. I recognized him. To say that Tommy Buechler. had his fingers in a lot of different pies would be a real understatement. In the already shaky world of Chicago politics, this man was an octopus. I'd never met him, but I'd seen his picture a bunch of times. He'd always been a little on the chunky side but in person he looked gaunt, and the gray skin on his face sagged.

"Come on, Pal," he said. "We're closing up now."

"Can I have another minute? I'm Henry Atwater from the Trib. I'm doing a story on Jake Wilson."

Buechler's face brightened." You with the press? That's different." He stuck out a hand. "Tommy Buechler. I own this dive."

I shook his hand and wondered why a guy like Buechler would want to own a place like this.

"Ain't that the best, damn blues you ever heard?" asked Buechler.

I couldn't argue with him there.

"That's why I brought him here," said Buechler. "I opened this place just for him. I'll send you the official bio. What's the number?"

"I was kind of hoping I could talk to Jake for a few more minutes."

"Impossible," he said, frowning. "Mr. Wilson has a previous appointment. Isn't that right, Jake?" He glanced sideways at Jake, who set down his beer, stood up, and strolled through a side door into his dressing room. Just like that.

I gathered my wits and turned back to Buechler. "So, business been pretty good, Mr. Buechler?" I asked.

"Call me Tommy," he said. "Everybody calls me Tommy." He flashed a weak smile, and his blue eyes sparkled for a moment. "You know how it is. It takes a while to build up a following. Write us a nice article. That will help."

I gave Tommy my number at the Trib and headed towards the door. I glanced back over my shoulder and saw Tommy walk through the same door Jake Wilson had gone through and close it behind him.

Later that evening I sat at my kitchen table, nibbling on kiwi fruit and rice. I popped a white pill and washed it down with pomegranate juice. I needed peak serotonin levels if I was going to write Jake Wilson the review he deserved. He should have been playing the Jordan Center, and if I had anything to say about it, he would.

I clicked on the wall screen and the rain forest filled up the room. I logged on and dictated my review, starting over several times until I had it just right. I sat back, satisfied. I had given it my best shot. Maybe it would bring in a crowd for Jake.

My brain was still racing from the pill, so I logged onto the Trib's database. Jake's bio said that he had been born in Amelia, Louisiana, so I ran a search of the birth records for the past 50 years. No Jake Wilson. Nothing in Terrabonne Parrish either.

He could have been using a stage name of course, or the whole bio could have been phony but I didn't think so. He seemed like the real thing, and besides, if you were going to come up with a stage name, you would probably come up with something a little more flashy than 'Jake Wilson.'

I planned to ask Buechler for a few more details the next night when I went back to see Jake. For the first time in my life, I had become a fan. I swallowed a black pill and headed off to bed as the rain forest winked off behind me.

The next night I had to stand in line at the club, even though light snow was falling. I squeezed through the door and grabbed one of the last available chairs, way back in the corner. Jake came out on stage and parked himself on his stool. He didn't say hello to the audience, didn't smile, nothing. He just started singing. Thankfully, the music was as good as I remembered from the night before, maybe even better.

I glanced back and saw Tommy Buechler leaning against the bar. He gave me a thumbs up. A waitress brought me a beer and said it was from Tommy.

After the show I waited for Jake to come to the bar, but he disappeared into his dressing room. As I stood to leave, Tommy came over and thanked me for the rave review.

"You're welcome here any time," he said.

"Don't mention it," I said. "The man deserves it."

"Yeah," said Tommy. "He's an original, all right."

There was something about Tommy's manner that made me nervous. His eyes kept darting back and forth like he was afraid that he would get busted any minute. I supposed that was normal when you lived a life like his.

I climbed the stairs and stood outside in the snow, my teeth chattering. The rest of the crowd had filtered away and I was alone on the sidewalk. A few cars purred by overhead, the whine of their engines muffled by the cold. The sounds of dance music wafted towards me from down the block but at this distance it was just a rumble of thumping bass notes.

I scanned the building. Was there a back door to this place? Would Jake come out that way? I put my hands in my pockets and strolled into the gangway. An alley cat hissed at me from a trashcan.

There was a door in the side of the building. I paced back and forth in front of it, feeling like a kid waiting outside Soldier Field for his favorite player to come out of the locker room.

The door opened and Jake Wilson stepped through, head down. He bumped into me and looked up. "You again," he said. "What you want?"

"I'm sorry if I startled you. Can I buy you a beer or something?"

"What for?"

"No special reason. I thought maybe we could talk. I wrote that review and..."

"That why all those people were there tonight? You write somethin' good?"

"Well, yeah."

"Thanks. That real nice but the man don't want me talkin' to nobody."

"Look, it won't take long. I know a place just down the block. The beer's real cold."

Jake looked back behind him, towards the door.

"Come on," I said. "Just for a few minutes. There's so much I'd like to ask you."

"I be a little thirsty," he answered. "Besides, I ain't nobody's *slave*."

The word slapped me in the face. Once upon a time somebody might have called *me* that but now it was just a word in the history books.

"Ummmm...okay, great," I said. "Let's go."

Michigan Avenue was busier than usual for a snowy night and it took us a while to find a place that wasn't jammed. We settled on Duffy's, my favorite little Irish place, and one of the few pubs in Chicago that hasn't yet given in to the virtual slots business, with its rows of flashing lights and the annoying sound of credit chips piling up in stainless steel trays. There's nothing but a mahogany bar, some comfortable booths, and Guinness on tap.

We took a booth in the corner and I ordered us a round. Evidently Jake had never had Guinness, because he coughed when he took his first sip and mumbled something about it tasting like tar. But he drank it down fast and we started on seconds.

"Where did you learn to play like that?" I asked. "From the old recordings?"

"Ain't had no recordings."

"Then who taught you? What program?"

"Ain't had no program."

"Then how did you learn?"

"I just do it, that's all. I sing from here." He pointed to his heart.

I couldn't argue with that.

We drank in silence as I tried to think of something else to ask.

"I wanna ax you something," he said.

I looked up. Jake had never initiated conversation before. He was starting to slur his words and I strained to understand his thick, bayou accent.

"Time," he said. "What you know about it?"

"What do you mean?"

"Travelin' in time. Goin' back. Or frontwards."

"Well, you know. Everyone knows. They have a few portals but the government keeps a really tight lid on them."

"Could they go back and kill somebody?"

I set down my beer. Why was he asking me this? "I guess somebody could," I answered, "but it's real illegal. If you killed somebody in the past you might screw up the present. That's why it's so controlled. But yeah, I suppose you could go back and bump somebody off. Theoretically. Why?"

Jake's hand gripped his glass until his knuckles turned white. "I gotta go," he said, and he stood up unsteadily.

"What? Wait, I'll take you in my car..."

But he was already gone.

Later that night I hit the databases again. My thinking was still a little fuzzy from the Guinness so I popped a purple hangover pill. Something smelled really bad here. I had called Louisiana that morning and no one I talked to had heard of a blues singer named Jake Wilson. I read as much as I could about Tommy Buechler. It seemed that he had connections in more places than just Chicago - my wallscreen lit up with six foot high pictures of Tommy with all kinds of famous people - entertainers, movie stars, rock stars, even the Prime Minister of Japan. I wondered how I hadn't run across Buechler before, because I'd met a lot of those people myself - except the Prime Minister of Japan, of course.

I shut off the screen and sat back. The pieces of the puzzle were coming together. I didn't like the picture they were starting to show.

The next night I showed up early at the Shady Gator and grabbed a seat up front. When Jake came out on stage he seemed afraid to look in my direction. It didn't affect his music, though. It was great as always, especially from the front row, and I found myself drifting back into that zone. Jake sang and the lyrics flowed out of him like smooth whiskey.

> *It's the last fair deal goin' down*
> *This the last fair deal goin' down, good lord*
> *On this Gulfport Island Road*
> *I'm workin' my way back home*

He eased into the solo, bending the B-string and coaxing a soft whimper out of the note, followed by a hammered G in the bass line. It was a beautiful touch that connected to something in my brain. Where had I heard that lick before, on that song?

I have an old recording at home. It's exceedingly rare, at least a hundred years old. It's *Last Fair Deal Gone Down* by Robert Johnson, still on vinyl, still in the original packaging. I never shared it with anyone, never transferred it over to data, nothing. It must be worth a lot of credits, but I've always kept it to myself. The recording has the same lick that Jake had just played.

Where had Jake learned it? From the same recording? That seemed impossible. There was only one explanation.

For once I wished the show were over. It was time to have a talk with Tommy Buechler.

Jake finished his last song and headed straight to his dressing room. I walked over to the bar as the crowd filed up the stairs. Tommy came out of the back room. I motioned him over.

"You're getting to be quite a fan," he said with his usual weak smile.

"You took him, didn't you?" I said.

"What?"

"Jake. You nabbed him."

Tommy's eyes flashed and the air turned to ice. I wasn't used to dealing with guys like this but I blundered forward.

"You know what I'm talking about," I said, spitting the words. "You got yourself a ride in a portal and you nabbed him."

Tommy's hands clenched and I thought he was going to haul off and punch me. Then, without looking away, he gave a quick, ominous flick of his wrist and the bartender went into the back room.

"What are you, a cop?" Tommy asked, holding me with his gaze.

"No."

"Then what's it to you?"

"He doesn't belong here. Can't you see that?"

Tommy snapped his fingers. "I could have you killed. *Just like that.*"

I should have foreseen this.

"Fine," I said, improvising. "Then the Trib will run my story."

"What story?"

"The one that will file automatically if I don't come home tonight."

Tommy hissed through his teeth. "I've got friends."

I didn't let up. "If there's even a *hint* that you broke the Time Laws, they'll be here in a heartbeat. Even you can't get away with something like that."

Tommy stared into my eyes for a long moment. Finally he turned away. His gaunt body seemed to deflate, and he suddenly looked very tired. "What did I get myself into?" he mumbled, looking down at the floor. There was a long pause as he gathered his wits. Then he stood up straight again.

"Okay," he said. "You wrote us a great review. I owe you one. So I'll give you some information. Off the record. And no cops."

I was amazed that he had given in so easily. He clearly wasn't the intimidating presence he might once have been. Now he looked like a tired, sick old man.

"We'll see," I answered.

Tommy cursed under his breath and then held one hand in the air, palm out. "God's honest truth," he said. "I nabbed him, just like you said. He was playing the Sweet Lips Lounge, Belmont and Halsted, August 25th, 1957. Can you believe that? It was over a hundred years ago. And I was *there*. We just wandered into the place. But I did know something about it. There was gonna be a fire in the club that night. Everyone was gonna die, including Jake. Charred beyond recognition. For once in my life I thought I had a chance to do something good for somebody before I kicked the…"

Tommy broke off and gazed at the stage. "You've heard him play," he said softly. "Wouldn't you have done the same thing?"

"But it's against the law," I said. "And for a very good reason. How'd you get on the portal?"

"Now that's something you don't need to know."

"Why Jake Wilson? Why not Beethoven or John Lennon or somebody like that?"

Tommy shrugged. "I didn't plan this ahead of time. We were there to witness the fire, a nice clean break, so we wouldn't change anything. But I didn't expect the music to be so…amazing. He never even did any recordings. It would have been lost forever."

"What if I spill the story?" I asked.

"You go ahead," Tommy said. "File your story. Then they'll come and get me. But they'll also come and get Jake. And they'll send him back. It's the law. And then he'll die. You might as well go stick a gun to the man's head right now and pull the trigger."

I wanted to rekindle my anger, to put my hands around Tommy's scrawny neck. But he had me.

"Did you threaten to go back and kill Jake's family?"

Tommy's eyes darted. "I had to tell him that. Otherwise he would have taken off. Can you imagine him wandering around a city that's a hundred years ahead of his time?"

"I'm leaving now," I said.

Tommy stood up and I thought he was going to block my path. But he just stepped aside. He must have been pretty confident that I wouldn't tell anybody. As I walked down Rush Street towards my car, I wondered if he was right.

That night I took a whole handful of pills. I felt like an accessory to a crime but what was I supposed to do?

I tried the databases. No one had kept very good records of poor blacks in Louisiana in the early 1900's. I found a Jake Wilson, born in Amelia in 1914. That was probably him. There were a few sketchy details about his life, but nothing else. I shut off the screen.

As I watched Jake perform the next night my heart ached for him. He sat up there and sang his guts out about losing everything and now I knew it was all real. But I just couldn't bring myself to even think about getting him sent back.

After the show I again waited for Tommy.

"Well?" he said.

"Well what?"

"No cops have been breaking down my door. I guess you didn't run that story."

"Not yet."

"Oh."

"Her name is Sally," I said quietly.

"What?"

"Sally. That's Jake's wife. The one he thinks you're going to go back and kill. I don't suppose you're really going to do that, are you?"

"No, of course not," Tommy admitted. "You don't know how many favors I used up the first time."

"I want to talk to Jake," I said. "He needs to know the truth. That's the only way I don't spill the beans."

Tommy looked like a trapped rat. "Okay," he finally muttered. "Tomorrow night. Jake gets here about an hour before show time. You can talk to him then."

All that night I couldn't sleep. I thought about my job. Was this what I was really meant to do? I had been at the Trib for twenty years. If I had ever had any passion for the music I reviewed it was long gone. Jake's music had brought some of it back but there was only one Jake. It would take a lot of pills to keep me doing this for twenty more years. I drifted off to sleep eventually, very late.

I walked into Jake's dressing room the next evening. It was a half-hour before show time and he sat alone, tuning his guitar. He didn't shy away from me so I guessed that Tommy had given him the okay. I pulled up a chair.

"I know what happened to you," I said.

"You mean how they come get me?" he asked.

"Yeah. But I think you should know something. Tommy Buechler isn't going to go back and kill anyone. He can't do that."

"You sure?" Jake's rheumy eyes opened a little wider.

"Promise," I said.

"That good," he said, and he leaned back in his chair. "So when can I go home? This ain't much of a place to be."

I knew that this question had been coming. How could I answer it? I decided on the truth.

"They could send you back. As of matter of fact, if anyone finds out where you came from, they have to send you back."

"Well alright," he said, his eyes brightening. "Sally be waitin' for me."

I paused, feeling hollow in my gut.

"You need to understand something," I said. "When they came and got you, they saved you from something that was gonna happen later that night. There was a fire and the Sweet Lips burned to the ground. Nobody got out alive. If you go back, you'll die too."

Jake pursed his lips. Sweat was running down his forehead even though the room was chilly. "But if I go back and know what happens, why can't I just leave *before* it happens?"

I sighed. "It doesn't work that way. You'd have no memory of being here, no memory of what I just told you, and everything would happen the way it was supposed to."

Jake squinted his eyes and he suddenly looked a lot older. I could see the wheels turning as he tried to understand.

"So I go back and I'm…dead?"

I nodded.

"And Sally…"

"She'll still be a widow."

There was a long, long pause. All I heard was Jake's raspy breathing and the rumble of the crowd gathering in the other room. Finally, Jake looked into my eyes.

"I ain't never goin' home no more?" he asked, his voice breaking.

"No," I answered."

There was another awkward pause as Jake looked down at the floor and shook his head.

"So I just another sad *slave,* standin' on the shore, lookin' cross the ocean, knowin' he can't swim."

There was that word again.

"I can check on your wife," I said. "To see how things turned out for her."

Jake lifted his head. "That be good," he whispered.

"And kids. Did you have any kids?"

"No," he muttered. "We were gonna have some but I guess we run out of time."

Jake stood up as the sounds of impatient clapping came from the other side of the door.

"What will you do now?" I asked.

"Sing the blues," he said. "Should be easy now."

"Jake?"

"What?"

"Could you teach me a few things? I have an old guitar from my grandfather."

"Old guitars is best," he said.

The clapping got louder. Jake wiped at his eyes. "Be here tomorrow night, after the show," he said, as he stepped through the door and out onto the stage. Applause erupted as the door closed behind him.

I stood up and took a clear plastic case out of my pocket. I opened the lid and grabbed a handful of colored pills. Clearly, I needed help and this should do it.

I stood there a moment staring at the bright colors in my hand. What would happen if I didn't take any pills? Would my head explode? Like everyone else, I'd relied on them for so long that it was hard to imagine a world without them. A world like the one that Jake had come from.

I knew it was crazy, and I knew I'd probably regret it. But at the last moment, instead of popping the pills into my mouth I tossed them into the toilet. Then I tipped up the case so the rest of the pills fell into the bowl as well.

The pills melted into the water in tendrils of bright, Easter egg colors. They swirled together until the water was a drab, dirty brown color. There was no bright orange, no purples, no reds. And no blues.

It was then that I knew what Jake Wilson had done. He had brought back some of the colors.

I flushed the toilet and the noise mingled with the sounds of the eight bar delta blues, coming through the dressing room door.

Wayne Faust *is a speculative fiction writer from Colorado, USA. He's had over 50 stories published in various places around the world. He's also been a full-time music and comedy performer for over 45 years, playing in 40 US States, and in England, Scotland, Holland, and Mexico. (www.waynefaust.com). From writing songs all those years, where you have to say everything you need to say in three verses or less, his prose tends to be tightly-written and fast-moving.*

The Great Hunt

Timothy Friend

I

If not for the money she owed the Tcharsov brothers, and their threat of a one-way trip to the bottom of the harbor if payment was further delayed, Moth wouldn't have agreed to the meet at all. Now that she was here, she was wondering if drowning might not be more pleasant.

For one thing, the heat was oppressive. Summers in the tiered city of Mahljar were always unpleasant, but down in the cramped streets and narrow alleys of the Gutter it was almost unbearable. Her other complaint was the wrinkled old horse's ass she was meeting. His name was Lord Gorra, he was from House Vetros, and he wouldn't shut up about her scars.

"Are they painful?"

Moth said, "Not anymore."

"They look painful."

"So stop looking."

"I tend to look a person in the eye when speaking to them. Impolite not to."

"But talking about my face," Moth said, "is the height of etiquette."

Moth had chosen the darkest corner of the tavern, kept the hood of her cloak up despite the heat, all in the hope of avoiding conversation about her burns. Yet here she was, listening to this prick tell her how bad her scars looked.

Gorra said. "How did it happen?"

Moth said, "What does it matter? You're not hiring me for my looks."

"I was merely surprised," Gorra said, "by the extent of your disfigurement."

Moth said, "You want, I can send you out of here with some scars of your own. You can be surprised every time you look in a mirror."

Gorra's eyes narrowed, and his voice went cold and flat. "I'm willing to tolerate your gruff demeanor, to a degree. But I'm still a highborn. Threaten me again and you'll spend the rest of your life rotting in a cell."

Moth slipped a hand into the pocket of her trousers, squeezed the small stone she kept there. The stone warmed against her palm, and she felt a slight tingle along her arm. A golden strand of light, visible only to Moth, traced Gorra's bodyguard, who sat alone at the next table.

I already know about that one, she thought. *Who else?*

The light ran along the floor, weaving through the sparse crowd. Two men at the bar stood out for their size and bulk. The light formed a glowing outline around both of them.

Moth nodded toward the closest bodyguard, and said, "You put too much stock in your men. If this lard-ass tries to lay hands on me, first thing I'll do is slit your throat. The pair at the bar? Too far away to stop me. Plus, they've been throwing back drinks since you arrived. Also, you may be highborn, but you're obviously not connected. You didn't even have the juice to make the City Protectors fetch me, had to come down to the Gutter yourself. So we can keep twitching until one of us decides it's time to jump, or you can tell me what you want."

"I want nothing more than what's rightfully mine. And you are going to help me reclaim it."

Rovann brushed a strand of damp red hair from her face and tried to concentrate on what the fat highborn was saying. There were no windows in the storeroom, and the heat made it hard to concentrate. Was he trying to hire her? That was absurd. He'd just caught her stealing.

She stole a glance at Gannet seated in the corner, a guard on either side of him. The scared and confused look on his face left Rovann sick with guilt.

They'd only met two weeks ago, and he'd been her spotter for less time than that. He was out of his element, but eager to learn, not to mention good in the sack, so she'd kept him around.

Things had been going well only minutes ago. Gannet pointed out the portly, well-dressed graybeard in the marketplace to Rovann, and the lift went without a hitch. She passed the heavy purse off to Gannet, already congratulating herself on a successful haul. Then she rounded the corner and found herself face to face with half a dozen personal guards from Uphill. They rushed her into a fabric merchant's back room where the graybeard, whose name she learned was Lord Hoga, stood waiting, along with a trembling and teary-eyed Gannet.

"They came out of nowhere," Gannet said. "I didn't know what to do."

Hoga said, "You keep quiet."

None of this would have happened if she'd just kept working for old Jorrd, helping him peddle his elixirs. If Gannet lost a hand, or worse, because of her, she'd never forgive herself.

Rovann said, "I'm not sure I understand what you want. I'm just a pick-pocket."

Hoga patted the purse hanging, once again, from his belt. "I'm well aware of your skills, but pick-pockets are plentiful as fleas in the Gutter. Perhaps no one has ever told you this, but beneath the rough-spun clothing, and that tangled rat's nest of hair, you are quite a beautiful woman. I won't be needing you to scale walls or scramble across rooftops. It's not that sort of job."

Rovann narrowed her eyes and said, "What sort is it?"

Hoga said, "Nothing salacious, I assure you. I'm merely pointing out that you being such an attractive young woman will make the job easier."

Rovann was well aware of how she looked. But you dressed to draw attention when you were peddling snake-oil, not when you were picking pockets. And while Hoga claimed that his interest in her was without salacious design, his lingering gaze suggested otherwise. Still, it seemed unlikely he'd gone to this much trouble just to get laid.

Rovann said, "You still haven't told me what the job is."

Hoga said, "I'm sure you've heard of The Great Hunt of House Vetros."

Rovann shook her head. Highborns were always giving ostentatious names to mundane events. The Tragic Ruined Breakfast of the Seven Houses. The Most Painful Hangnail of House Vetros. The more boring the event the more grand the title.

Hoga said, "It was many years ago. I was with my cousins, Bort and Gorra, tracking a hill-cat that had been killing sheep. We were fifteen summers old, and it was our first hunt."

Hoga's voice took on a tone that suggested a long story, full of nostalgia and digressions into the lore of House Vetros. Rovann wiped a sleeve across her brow.

Gods and gold, was it possible all of his talk was actually making the room hotter? She wished he would just get to the point.

"The point is," Gorra said, "it was my kill, despite Hoga's claims to the contrary. But Hoga's monstrous ego would never allow him to admit that his shot had missed. And Bort, a cowardly lick-spittle even then, didn't have the dragon-stones to speak in my defense. In the end, for the sake of unity in the house, our fathers decided that Bort would keep the trophy. It's been in his possession for the last forty years, and now that he's dead, I want it."

Moth said, "You want me to steal it."

"Tomorrow night, during the Gathering of Mourners. Before the inventory of his home is conducted and turned over to his son."

Moth said, "That soon? I don't even know how I'll get in."

"Getting in won't be a problem," Hoga said. "It's getting out that will put your skills to use."

Rovann said, "If I refuse?"

Hoga gestured to Gannet, and said, "Then I'm afraid I will have to formally demand justice for House Vetros. I doubt the courts will take more than an arm. Or two."

Rovann avoided looking at Gannet. She said, "If I agree, what next?"

Hoga smiled and said, "Why, next we go shopping."

II

It was balmy Uphill, for which Rovann was grateful. Seated in Lord Hoga's carriage, feeling the night air on her face, it would have been easy to forget the Gutter even existed if not for the faint smell of garbage carried on the breeze.

The line of carriages stretched all the way up the cobblestone street and around the corner. Rovann drew another labored breath and hoped they would arrive soon. She couldn't take sitting much longer. Her new dress, in addition to being the most gorgeous and expensive piece of clothing she'd ever worn, was also the most uncomfortable. It was tight and restrictive, and it pinched in places she felt shouldn't be pinched.

Rovann had assumed a scented bath and a new dress were all she would need to fit in at the event, but upon being turned over to Hoga's fleet of servants yesterday she discovered how painfully wrong she'd been. She was soaked, sanded, oiled and powdered, manicured, pedicured, and plastered with make-up. Her hair was aggressively washed, detangled, ironed and then tightly braided and wound into a coil atop her head. The experience left her feeling raw from scalp to sole.

Lord Hoga sat across from her in the carriage, the ceremonial rapier he wore at his waist jutting up at an awkward angle. He hadn't spoken since they'd left for the gathering, and now that Rovann was dressed in highborn attire she noticed he didn't feel as free to ogle her, instead stealing quick glances when he thought she wasn't looking. Somehow that seemed worse than his blatant staring.

Upon arriving at the estate the carriage door was opened by an attendant. Hoga stepped out first and spoke quietly, muttering the name Lesto as he gestured toward Rovann. Lesto was the Lord she was here to represent. At least that was what she was supposed to say should anyone inquire. This Lord was apparently such the black sheep of House Vetros that his sending an unescorted female to represent him at a formal event warranted little more than an eye roll from the attendant.

Rovann took hold of Hoga's right arm in just the manner he'd shown her. Fingertips touching the back of his elbow, thumb flat against her palm. These were, she'd learned, the indicators that Hoga was chaperoning her strictly as a matter of house obligation. It seemed that the Seven Houses had no end of needlessly complex rituals. Rovann was grateful she wouldn't need to maintain her charade for long.

The entire ruse existed solely for the purpose of preserving Hoga's reputation. Should Rovann be caught in the act, Hoga would merely look like an old fool who had been taken advantage of by a deceitful beauty. The worst he would face was embarrassment. For Rovann though, it would be a swift trip to the executioner's block.

Hoga steered her through the foyer and along a short hallway to a cavernous ballroom where the attendees converged. When she stepped through the arched doorway, Rovann had to stifle a gasp at the grandeur of Lord Bort's mansion. With polished marble underfoot, elaborate tapestries lining the walls, and bejeweled highborns jammed shoulder to shoulder, Rovann felt overwhelmed by the sheer volume of wealth on display.

Rovann noted that there wasn't much mourning at this Gathering of Mourners. While no one had gone so far as to actually break into dance, it was clear no one was grieving. There was much laughter into cupped palms, servants rushing quietly about to refill wine glasses, and a general air of muted revelry. It felt, to Rovann, a bit like a party trying not to wake its sleeping host.

As they stood at the edge of the crowd, Hoga met Rovann's eyes and gave a nod. He moved away then, shaking hands and smiling at other guests as he slid his considerable bulk between closely huddled bodies with an ease Rovann wouldn't have thought possible without the application of butter.

It was time to go to work.

Rovann kept her eyes down as she exited the crowd and stepped into the hallway. With everyone in the ballroom, the rest of the mansion had the air of an abandoned museum. Statues and artwork, the value of which Rovann couldn't begin to guess, adorned the walls and lined the hallways. The many small, but expensive looking items on display made her lament her lack of pockets and curse the impractical nature of highborn fashion.Rovann turned down another hallway which, aside from different artwork adorning the walls, looked exactly like the previous one. She hoped she was remembering Hoga's directions correctly. She couldn't afford to get lost. In addition to the trophy she also needed to find a servant with a blue cravat.After several minutes of roaming Rovann came to Bort's den. The room was dim, with only the pale light of the moon coming in through a high window. Mounted animal heads hung from every available space on all four walls. Jungle cats, huge reptiles, fish and fowl, all staring down at Rovann with fixed, glassy eyes. She stood in the center of the room and looked about. How could possibly find a lone hill-cat head among all these others.

She surprised herself when she spotted it right away. It was sitting on a bookshelf behind the oaken desk instead of hanging on a wall. It was significantly smaller than the others.

A child's trophy, Rovann thought.

From behind her a voice said, "May I be of any assistance to the lady?"

Rovann jumped at the sound. She turned and saw a tall man standing in the doorway. He was a handsome fellow with dark hair, going gray at the temples. But more importantly, he wore a blue cravat, the symbol of a high ranking servant.

Rovann put her wrist to her forehead and said, "Oh, you gave me a start."

The man bowed his head. "My apologies."

Rovann didn't know what to say next. The surrounding severed heads pulled at her attention.

The servant, observing her unease, glanced up at the trophies and said, "Lord Bort was fond of the kill."

Rovann could only nod.

The man said, "May I escort the lady back to the gathering? The new lord has asked that the guests restrict themselves to the ballroom during the transition."

Rovann said, "I understand. It's just that I wasn't feeling well, and I wanted to find a place to sit quietly. I must have gotten lost."

The man eyed her curiously, but said nothing. He stepped to the side and extended his arm and gestured toward the hallway. Rovann allowed the man to lead her a few steps before leaning on him heavily and stumbling over her feet. The man caught her before she could fall. He helped her regain her balance, then guided her into a small alcove where he sat her on a velvet-covered stool.

Rovann said, "I suppose I'm still feeling poorly. I just need to catch my breath."

The man said, "The lady can rest here as long as she wishes."

She took this to mean he would leave her alone. But the servant merely stepped back and clasped his hands behind him, waiting.

Rovann said, "May I trouble you for some water?"

The man said, "I'll fetch it right away."

As the servant stepped away from her, Rovann said, "Thank you. You're very kind."

The man stopped and slowly turned back to Rovann. He looked at her closely, scrutinizing her. She could sense her efforts at passing for a highborn were failing.

The man said, "The new lord is a little shit, worse than his father. Not that it matters as he'll be staffing the place with his own servants. I'll be out of a job as of tomorrow, with no prospects. My reward for thirty years of service."

Rovann stared, uncertain what she should say.

The man said, "I'm merely informing you that my concern for what happens within these walls is diminishing by the moment. Perhaps knowing this will help the lady catch her breath. I'll fetch that water now."

He turned on his heel and strode away.

A weight seemed to vanish from Rovann's chest, and she drew a deep breath. When the servant was out of sight she looked down at the key she now held in her open palm. Given his attitude she thought it possible she could have just asked for it. But she doubted his lack of concern extended to blatantly aiding a thief. Rovann got to her feet and hurried back to the den.

Moth slipped quietly over the window sill and dropped to the floor. It was a longer drop than she'd guessed and she landed more loudly than intended. She froze, anticipating a rush of guards at any moment, but none came.

Moth stood from her crouch and surveyed the room. This Bort fellow sure liked dead things. Moth almost whistled aloud at the sight of all the animal heads, but caught herself.

She thought, *Damn you, Gorra. All of your chatter and you didn't think to mention there are a hundred other heads on the wall?*

Moth scanned the rows of trophies. She hadn't accounted for being unable to find what it was she'd been sent to steal, and the longer she spent in the house the more frustrated she grew.

After taking in the room Moth closed her eyes for a moment. When she opened them again she let her gaze drift lightly, never landing anywhere in particular, but searching for anything that stood out to her.

The chair behind the desk. It sat at an odd angle, as if someone had moved it out of the way. As far as Moth could tell there was nothing behind the chair, just an empty shelf.

The only bare shelf in the room, she thought.

Moth palmed the stone in her pocket, feeling it warm to her touch. A line of light appeared on the floor. It glowed strongly. Someone had been in here very recently. The line traced a path from the hallway halfway into the room, then turned and went back out the door without going near the desk.

Moth cursed in frustration.

All at once the trail of light shot back into the room, around the desk to the now empty shelf, then abruptly back across the room and out the door again.

Moth released the stone and, quickly as she dared, scaled the shelves back up to the window through which she'd entered. Outside, slowly fading even as it moved across the lawn, was the line of golden light headed in the direction Moth had come from.

Rovann thought for sure she would be spotted as she awkwardly lugged the mounted hill-cat head across the lawn. She was moving as fast as she could, but between the trophy, the lantern and matches she'd stolen from Bort's den, and the short strides imposed by her dress, it was slow going. It took her several minutes to reach the far edge of the estate, where large stones jutted out of the ground to form a natural boundary.

A heavy iron gate stood between two of the stones. Rovann set the trophy on the ground in anticipation of unlocking the gate, but when she went to slide the key into the latch she discovered it was already unlocked and swung easily open.

On the other side of the gate a tunnel descended gently into the dark. Rovann had long heard stories of the caves that criss-crossed beneath Mahljaar. Supposedly they had been used for smuggling, and that was how the Seven Houses had originally made their fortunes. That had been over a hundred years ago, during the Vikalian occupation, and the entrances had long since been sealed. It was whispered that some highborns still used the caves for their own purposes. The tunnels were labyrinthine, and it was dangerous to venture into them without a map. Possession of a map was even more dangerous as the price for being caught with one was hanging.

Rovann lit a match and put it to the candle in her lantern, then retrieved the trophy before pulling the gate closed behind her. When it failed to latch she took a moment to examine the lock and found a small pebble jammed in the mechanism.

That was curious. Had Lord Hoga set this up for her? If so, why did he instruct her to steal the key? Regardless, she decided, it was best to cover her trail. She plucked the pebble free and slammed the gate closed.

Next she spent a full minute struggling to lift her tight dress high enough to reach the folded map tucked in her garter. In a moment of sudden frustration Rovann took hold of the hem and ripped the dress all the way to her hip.

Rovann wondered what Hoga would say, considering what he'd paid for the dress. *That's what you get,* she thought, *for not giving me pockets.*

Moth kicked at the locked gate in fury. What was going on here? Who the hell was she following?

Moth considered this as she pulled the small set of picks from her pocket and set to work on the lock. It took her several minutes to get the gate open, which made her grateful she wasn't being pursued. Once inside the tunnel Moth retrieved the lantern she'd left hidden among the rocks and lit it. With the lantern in one hand, and the other clutching the stone in her pocket, she started into the tunnel. She could've used the map Gorra had given her, but there was always the chance it could be misread. Better to just follow her own trail back the way she'd come.

As she walked she thought, *When I catch this other thief, I'm going to lay a beating on him he'll never forget.*

Rovann stared into the abyss. This couldn't be right.

With the trophy under her arm she held the map in one hand and the lantern in the other. She thought she'd followed the correct path, only to end up at the edge of this black pit.

Maybe she could find her way back to the entrance and then walk down the Gutter. The Uphill streets were heavily patrolled, but she liked her chances up there better than down here. This was like she was running a maze blindfolded.

A sound behind her caused Rovann to turn and step back in alarm at the sight of a black-clad figure standing very close. Her foot came down on empty air. Rovann gasped, feeling herself going over the edge, tipping back into that black nothingness. She spun her arms wildly, trying to regain her balance and sent the lantern, the map, and the trophy plummeting into the dark.

A hand reached out, grabbed her arm, and pulled Rovann roughly back to solid ground.

Rovann stepped quickly away from the ledge on shaky legs while the darkly dressed figure took her place staring down into the void. Rovann could see it was a woman. She was short and wiry, no more than five feet tall, dressed in gray trousers and tunic along with a lightweight hooded cloak that was black as night. She carried a lantern of her own, and with the hood down Rovann could see that the woman had been badly burned sometime in the past. Her face was mottled pink and gray, with the rough texture of cured reptile hide. The skin around her mouth was puckered and wrinkled like that of an old crone, but Rovann guessed her to be close to her own twenty-eight years. The woman's short dark hair looked like it had been cut with a dull blade, and there was a white streak running back from her left temple. The woman turned away from the ledge and looked at Rovann with sea-blue eyes full of rage.

The woman said, "What the hell did you do that for?"

Rovann said, "You startled me."

The woman said, "So you just threw it into the pit?"

Rovann said, "I didn't throw it. I dropped it. And what's it to you?"

"It was mine."

"Yours?"

"Well, it was supposed to be mine. Until you came along and stole it."

Rovann said, "That sort of makes it mine, doesn't it. I'm surprised there's a second thief who wanted the thing."

The scarred woman made a dismissive sound. "Second thief? Hardly. I'm the first thief. The one true thief. The king of fucking thieves."

The woman said, "I didn't mean it like that. It isn't a competition."

"Damn right it's not. And who the hell are you? You might have fooled those idiots up there, but you're no highborn."

"Rovann Emerus. Butcher's Corner, born and raised. And you?"

The woman said, "Moth."

Afer a moment Rovann realized no other information was forthcoming. She said, "Moth? You mean, <u>the</u> Moth? The one and only Moth?"

"So you've heard of me."

"Of course not, you arrogant ass."

Moth's damaged features abruptly cracked into a broad smile. "You surprise me."

"How's that?"

"Your first choice for an insult wasn't a remark about my face."

Rovann said, "Wasn't your face that was aggravating me."

Moth laughed out loud. "C'mon. We've got a long walk. We can swap stories about a couple of highborn jackasses and a pair of thieves dumb enough to work for them."

III

They had been walking for over an hour and Moth figured they had to be getting close to the entrance. She still didn't know how she would settle her debt to the Tcharsov brothers. Laying low wasn't really an option. She stood out no matter where she went.

Moth looked over at Rovann. The woman was not what she'd expected when she set out in pursuit. Even in her current disheveled state Rovann could almost pass for an Uphill resident. Her perfectly sculpted face, along with her flawless alabaster skin, were truly breathtaking. It was only the way she carried herself that betrayed her. She lacked the haughty, disdainful attitude of a true highborn.

Rovann said, "You know your way around these tunnels pretty well."

Moth pulled the stone from her pocket long enough to show it to Rovann, then put it back. Rovann gaped in astonishment.

She said, "A dragon-stone? I thought only wizards had those."

Moth didn't answer.

They rounded a bend in the tunnel and came to a wide space that seemed to be a junction for several other tunnels branching off in different directions. Directly in front of them three figures stirred in the shadows. Moth pulled her hand from her pocket and drew her dagger.

A lantern flared, revealing Lord Gorra and his two biggest bodyguards. Moth kept her dagger in her hand.

Gorra said again, "Who is this woman? And where is my damn trophy. Don't trifle with me, you scar-faced bitch."

Moth glanced at Rovann, said, "See what I mean. Always the face."

Moth noticed that the two bodyguards had their short-swords drawn.

Moth said, "Any particular reason you and your boys are waiting here in the dark?"

Gorra said, "I was…I was anxious to receive my prize and thought I would save you the trouble of bringing it to me."

Moth said, "I don't see a purse tied to your belt. How were you going to pay me? You carrying those gold coins up your ass? Or were you maybe planning to ambush me?"

Before Gorra could answer, a light flared in one of the side tunnels and then another highborn carrying a lantern stepped into the open. This one was fat, with a thick gray beard. He and Gorra exchanged surprised looks.

Gorra said, "Hoga. What are you doing here, you bloated pig?"

Hoga said, "As if you didn't know, you bastard."

Hoga turned to Rovann. "Where is it?"

Rovann said, "I lost it."

Gorra and Hoga both said, "You lost it?"

Rovann nodded.

Moth said, "She did. I saw it."

Hoga said, "I won't pay for something twice, so if this is some feeble attempt to extort more money from me it won't work. That trophy is rightfully mine, and I mean to have it."

Gorra said, "I'll see you dead first."

Upon hearing this Hoga placed his lantern on the ground and drew his rapier. Gorra did the same and the pair went at each other with a ferocity that belied their ages. With no instructions from their master, the two bodyguards decided to do the job they'd been brought to do. They raised their swords and came at Moth.

Moth threw her lantern and one of the men swatted it away with his sword. The other man lunged and forced Moth to back away. They came on fast.

She ducked a swing from a short sword and deflected a lunge from another with the flat of her blade. The impact jarred her wrist and almost knocked the dagger from her hand.

Moth believed she could've taken one of them, but with both of them, and her back against the wall, she knew she was only buying time. And not much of that.

Rovann crouched against the wall of the tunnel and watched Moth, amazed at the woman's speed. She was a shadowy blur as she ducked and twisted, narrowly avoiding death with every movement. The sound of steel on steel filled the space and pressed down on Rovann as if trying to hold her in place. But the sight of Moth fighting so viciously emboldened her, and she stood up in spite of her fear.

Rovann looked about desperately, hoping to find a loose rock or dropped weapon she might be able to use. There was nothing, and even if there were she knew she was unlikely to spot it in the weak light from Hoga's lantern.

The lantern.

Hoga and Gorra, their swords locked, snarled and swore at one another as they shuffled closer to Rovann. She gave Hoga a shove that sent them both staggering, then hurried to the lantern and kicked it down the tunnel.

Everything went black.

When the light went out Moth dove to the ground. She'd seen Rovann kick the lantern, but couldn't grasp why. Then she got it.

Moth reached into her pocket, grasped the stone. A second later she saw a pair of glowing outlines cutting two man shaped figures from the darkness. She leaped to her feet, plunged her dagger into the black forms and watched them fall.

Moth waited quietly in the dark.

The other two, she thought.

Moth saw the familiar outline appear around two figures on the ground. Hoga and Gorra, each of their rapiers piercing the other's heart.

Idiots.

Moth said, "You okay?"

From out of the dark she heard, "Yeah. You?"

"Yeah. That was quick thinking. You saved my ass."

"I owed you."

Moth said, "So did Gorra. But I don't think I'll be getting paid."

Rovann said, "I think I can help with that."

IV

It took some effort to locate him. In the short time they'd known each other they had always met at her place, so she'd never found out where he lived. It turned out his room was above a laundry not far from Market Square.

Rovann entered his room in a rush, smiling broadly, as if eager to see him.

It was early and Gannet was still in bed. He bolted upright, rubbing at his face. "Rovann. I…I was so worried about you."

She had changed out of her dress and back into her own clothes. Gannet got out of bed and crossed the room to her, his eyes innocent and wide. As she observed his naked form, Rovann found herself hoping she was wrong.

Rovann said, "I'm fine. I'm just glad Lord Hoga let you go."

Gannet was flustered, but recovering fast. He said, "Yes, well, I suppose he didn't see any need to keep me. What with you off doing his dirty work and all."

Rovann said, "That reminds me. Hoga gave me the rest of what he owed you." She held up a small velvet purse and tossed it to Gannet who caught it one-handed.

Gannet said, "That's surprising. I thought I'd seen all I would ever get from that..." He tipped the bag into his hand and filled his palm with stones. Gannet looked up at Rovann, his guileless expression all at once replaced by cold cunning.

He said, "Clever. I walked right into that. What gave me away?"

Rovann said, "It was Hoga who slipped up. Tell me, was this the plan from the beginning?"

Gannet shrugged. "It was just business. Hoga has a taste for Gutter women, and I procure his entertainment."

Rovann said, "You're a pimp."

Gannet smirked, said, "If you like. I've been called worse.

Hoga told me about his plan, the special qualities he wanted in a thief, so I sought you out. I think he was waiting for an anniversary or some other event, but then that Bort fellow died and he got in a mad rush. We arranged for Hoga to be in the market, and for me to play the sad puppy once he had laid hands on you."

Rovann said, "I appreciate your being so forthcoming. I'll be on my way now, just as soon as you pay me."

Gannet laughed.

Rovann said, "I'm serious. If you're smart you'll hand it over. Every coin. I don't share my earnings with a pimp."

Gannet's eyes went cold and dead. He lunged and grabbed a handful of Rovann's hair in his fist. "And I don't share with anyone. Any of my other girls can tell you that."

There was a thump from the other side of the room as Moth slipped over the windowsill and tumbled to the floor. She was on her feet and moving closer when Gannet turned around.

He said, "Gods and gold, who the hell is this ugly-"

Moth's lead-weighted sap caught him across his jaw and spun him around. She landed a second blow on the back of his head and he fell to the floor and didn't move.

A hasty search and Rovann located the bag of coins from Hoga. She tossed it to Moth.

Rovann said, "Will this cover your debt?"

Moth nodded.

Rovann said, "You should stay away from the roulette table."

Moth sighed. "If only I would." She pointed down at Gannet. "He's still breathing. Do you want me to..." She drug a finger across her throat.

Rovann said, "No. I don't want to have to dispose of the body."

Moth said, "Yeah, that is a bother. So what do you intend to do next?"

Rovann said, "Anything, so long as it doesn't involve highborns."

Moth said, "It's too bad you feel that way. You see, I have this map..."

Timothy Friend is the author of the Brittle and Ashe series, and Rocket Ryder and Little Putt-Putt Go Down Swinging. His fiction has appeared in Mythic, Crossed Genres and Pulp Modern. You can find out more at www.timothyfriend.net.

Lost to the Dark

Frances Koziar

I have forgotten her name.

I have forgotten many things, but as the years have passed, that I have forgotten her name has come to bother me the most. She was only a baby when I was captured, her name just one word of many that wife spoke before I left for the battle, only one word, so easily forgotten when my screams drowned out the world. When they stretched me, cut me, burned me, her name had seemed the least of my losses.

I have forgotten the scent of my wife, of spring, of anything that isn't blood and sweat, mold and faeces and urine. I have forgotten the sound of laughter that isn't cruel or mad, of birdsong, of wind through the long grasses of home. Instead I know screams and dripping water, and the heavy silence of soldiers forgotten and waiting to die in dungeons beneath the earth.

But twenty years later, as I wake early from a dream that feels like the life I once knew—close and yet I can't remember—it is my daughter's name I want to remember the most. Because somewhere out there she is alive, and it is her world now. I stare up at the ceiling I know so well, tracing its cracks like a map out of this labyrinth, or a map to answers, because maybe answers are the only thing we can still reach down here. I sit up, and a sigh escapes me.

We were soldiers once. Stupid, ignorant men and women and non-binary folk fighting in a civil war we had lost. They had forgotten us, I had decided years ago. They must have forgotten us. The torture had stopped, but they hadn't freed us. We would rot in these cells that had become as much part of ourselves as our scarred, near-naked bodies and the phantoms that haunted us in the night.

Trayan starts doing pushups in the cell across the battered stone floor from mine, and I shift into position to copy zer. We thought ze was crazy at first, in those early years, doing exercises in the morning, and then a series of Takan-knows-what activities throughout the day like a noble with appointments, but now we all do it. Not for long—we aren't fed enough for that—but we all do the exercises together in the silence that we spend so much of our time in. When first meal comes—we get two: one late in the morning and one late in the afternoon—it is one of the three meals the guards alternate between: a ball of rice bread, a bowl of beans, and two slices of a pink citrus fruit.

"Swap," Enellen says from the cell next to mine, but I am already moving to our shared wall. I am in the last cell of our hall—Trayan too, across the way—and Enellen is to my right. She reaches her hand out through the front bars of her cell, snakes her arm around the wall dividing us, and takes the ball of rice bread I hold out. I take her bowl in exchange, dump half of her beans into my bowl, and then return the other half, as always.

"Cut his hair," she says, referring to the guard who had just delivered our meals.

"Looks younger," I rasp, using my voice for the first time since the day before.

We eat.

Enellen and I speak to each other. That is all one can say in such a place. We are not friends. There is no love. But we speak to one another.

"New guard," she says, seeing her before I do. When a new guard comes to take our bowls—we all push them out obediently, well trained since a time we don't remember—I see that she is young, with fierce dark eyes that see more than is necessary in such a place. There is nothing, I muse, to see. We are the same. The place is the same. For years at a time, the guards are the same. Someone must hire them. Someone must tell them to take care of us, to feed us, to clean our cells once a week while we are shackled, but that someone, I muse too, might be the only one who remembers us.

This is not a bad thing. When we were remembered, we were tortured. Tortured for supporting the wrong side. Tortured for secrets we didn't know. Tortured just for the fun of rubbing defeat in our faces. But there is something that seeps into your mind over the years when you are forgotten. Like damp air settling onto stone and metal, changing it, rusting it, molding it, hiding how things used to be.

And eventually, it will drive you mad.

Maybe we are already there, Enellen and Trayan and I. I am not sure if I will be able to tell. Some go suddenly, but others change over the years, bit by bit, until there's nothing left of the person they once were. One person used to sing, a few cells down, but he doesn't anymore. One used to talk too much, and now ze doesn't speak at all. A third is always speaking, as if speaking is the only thing keeping her alive. Speaking in a desperate way, mumbled words that will drive you mad if you listen, speaking even when we try to sleep, like the steady hum of a broken machine.

It is cleaning day, a day that feels social and eventful to me. We are let out one by one, starting with Trayan and I. Our wrists our shackled, and we are led in pairs out of the hall we never otherwise leave and into a large bare room. We are shackled side by side to a wall while the guards go back for the others. Once we are all in line, some guards clean our rooms while the others clean us one by one.

Trayan is unshackled first, as always, stripped and made to stand on the drain. The two guards left scrub him as he stands there and shifts when they need zer to.

At the beginning, we fought. At the beginning we spoke passionately, we plotted escape, we shouted hate back at the guards who spat in our faces.

Now we are like old horses, too old or too wise or too broken to do anything but plod along obediently. We all remember pain, and we all know that nothing is worth it. While everything else fades, that is the one thing we can't forget.

In my old life, I was of the Builder's Guild, and specialized in making buildings of stone. My wife and I had our own outside the city, at the edge of the great plains. When the princess had passed through seeking soldiers, speaking of money and pride, of defending our way of life from the lawlessness of the new mages and the queen's rule, she had promised that she would protect us in the same way that we would protect our country. She had promised that we would stand together, no matter what.

It is my turn. I am unfastened from the wall, led to the drain. The cloth around my crotch is untied and tossed away to be washed properly. Water is dumped on me, cold and shocking. I don't move as the two guards scrub my body roughly, but with the skill of long practice. One of them looks twenty years my senior—or would if we hadn't all aged at least ten years in our first couple—and is perhaps sixty-five, while the other is the younger man who just cut his hair who has only worked with us for the past six years. The new young woman I'd seen earlier was with the group cleaning the cells. Depending on the occasion and time of day, there would be four to six guards on duty at once, a detail I knew as much because the guards were something I had stared at for more hours than I could count like everything else, as because I had once memorized such details, when I had still hoped to escape in that time so long ago that my memories have faded to colourlessness.

Now, I wonder if I would even recognize the outside world, or it me. I have an image of my wife with our babe in her arms standing in front of our house as I rode away, and though I know that that image is no longer true, it is still what I think of when I think of the outside world, in moments when I am crazy enough to imagine or wonder. And I think, so many years later, that I would not prefer the reality.

Just as I am being led back to the wall, a fresh wrap around my bony waist, there is a muffled cry from the hallway. I look that way blankly as I offer my hands to be re-shackled. The guard—the older one—does so, before ze steps back and pauses to watch the younger one leave to investigate what happened.

Someone fell, I think, hardly paying attention. I close my eyes and enjoy the wetness and raw cleanliness of my skin, feel the stone, now slippery, beneath my calloused feet.

"They're supposed to be cleaning us," Allaya—the woman who always speaks—is mumbling, her voice the only well-used one amongst us, "*but who can be clean in darkness, in stone? What if we mold like the stones, wash away like the blood? Bathing, we are always bathing in the past, in the nightmares—*" A hesitation. "*Different. It's cleaning day—*"

I sense the change like a gentle wind against my skin, a change in the others beside me that is only audible from that barest, shocking hesitation in Allaya's constant murmuring.

I open my eyes.

In the doorway stands the new guard: the young woman, eyes burning now, blood dripping from the sword in her hand and splashed across her armour. A giant of a man I have never seen before comes up behind her, as does a scrawny, lanky person that makes me think *thief* just to look at zer.

"And you?" the woman asked the older guard—the only one, I realize with the sluggishness of bog-water, that is still alive.

Ze lifts zer hands and takes half a step backward—no fear, no anger, just the same steadiness that we have all become used to—and the woman hesitates. Then she lowers her sword, and looks at us, standing in a row, unmoving.

I watch her, and I feel nothing as she studies at us for a moment and then nods to her smaller companion. Twenty years ago, I think as the thief begins unlocking us one by one starting at the far end, I would have known what to do. Now, I only feel a budding unease in my chest that for the first time in twenty years, I don't know what is happening.

"We're getting you out of here," the woman tells us, and for a moment, her words sound even more insane than Allaya's. "Are there any more of you?" she asks when we say nothing, staring at our neat line of twenty-two, no one having moved even a step.

We don't even know this. We know our hallway, but we don't know if there are other hallways, or how many, don't know if other prisoners were killed or kept, don't know anything beyond our daily nothings. For a moment there is a silence, filled only with Allaya's husky voice.

"Why are there people? Why are there different people? Why are there guards who aren't guards? You shouldn't kill the guards. We shouldn't hurt them, or they'll hurt us. They always hurt us. They hurt us too much..."

"Maybe it's too late," the lanky one says, zer young grave eyes sweeping along our line.

"Let's get them out of here," the giant man says briskly, and he starts to wave us along. "This way," he says, and—nudged along—we obediently begin walking.

We walk in order, of course, which requires us to snake around, Trayan in the lead, me second, Enellen fourth. The young woman, the leader of whoever these people are, stands to the side as we pass her, her eyes passing back and forth along us as if she is looking for answers. In her, I see nothing that I know. I see brightness and energy. I see fire and anger. I see shock and determination.

We are led into another hall, one I must have seen once before, but have no recollection of. I remember that I was brought here violently. I remember jeers, remember shame, remember being beaten. I do not remember the hallways.

We climb stairs until we leave the dungeon entirely. When I step out onto the fur of a rug, I stop, unable to comprehend, unable to continue and not sure if I even want to.

"Keep going," the man, the warrior, says to me, pushing me slightly. I take a couple more halting steps until I stand beside Trayan, and then I stop again. I am staring at the rug—red-brown and furry like nothing I have felt in twenty years. The others pool behind me like logs hitting a damn, and Allaya begins talking about colour and light.

When I realize Trayan is not looking at the rug but is looking up, I follow zer gaze to a room filled with things I don't know, and a room filled with dead bodies. The smell of blood I know too well, but not the smells of fresh air and cleanliness, nor the sounds of voices and unfettered movement, and—somewhere in the distance—birdsong.

There are other soldiers here, others who work for the woman who has rescued us, standing amongst the carnage.

Why? I wonder at last. *Why did someone want to rescue us?*

And an older, strangled voice: *Why now?*

"You are my father," the young woman says, suddenly at my side. She says it half in question, staring at the dark brown birthmark stained across the light brown skin of my thigh, poking out from under my wrap.

I can do nothing but stare. I cannot think. I cannot understand. I cannot wonder.

"Captain. Valeis," says one of the soldiers, coming up behind her. Others look to Valeis for instructions, but she stares at me. Looking, perhaps, for recognition I cannot give.

"Isolan," I rasp at last, the first of us—beyond Allaya—to say anything. "My wife."

The young woman—twenty years old—steps forward and hugs me gently. I don't move, because moving always makes it worse. I close my eyes, ready for the shattering, mind-bending pain that is all I remember can come from touch.

But then Valeis steps back, her eyes glimmering—the same greeny brown as her mother's, I remember suddenly and disorientingly—and abruptly turns away. She gives sharp order to the others. *Take them outside. Check for others. Send word to Lord Farnaras.*

Each line is incomprehensible, but the last one sticks like a bur as we are led across the room. *Farnaras. Farnaras. Farnaras.*

And then I remember, as if some other man's memories have been leant to me out of pity. Farnaras was the son of the princess I had worked for. The princess who left us all here.

Her son had disagreed, I thought, the notion coming from a detached part of my brain that was running nonstop, speaking with the same restless desperation as Allaya mumbling behind me.

"Lights and bodies and lights and bodies and not our home. Where did we go? We aren't here. We aren't there. They aren't here," she mutters, her breath nearly brushing my bare neck.

"Who are they? Why do they move us on cleaning day? My wrap is dirty. Scratchy, scratchy. No colour. Wrong room. No shadow. Should be shadow. We live in shadow. Blinding. Chase away the ghosts. Why a door?" she asked as we cross the room and near a huge rounded set of wooden doors, pure light burning along the open crack between them like the heart of a fire. *"Where's the hallway? I want a hallway. Walking, walking. Not far enough; too far. Go back to sitting. Sitting all day, quiet and moving. Why are we dying? Why are they dead?"*

I shouldn't listen, I learned that long ago, but Allaya's words only feel like my fears spoken aloud—mad and distorted and nonsensical but still very much there. I don't want to go out. I'm not ready to go out. I don't even remember the world.

I hear the whisper of steel and remember the pummel of a sword knocking me dead, remember red-hot pokers and the laughter of men who never come anymore, and I spin around.

I see Trayan darting back from a soldier as lithely as if ze had been training as one all these years, rather than just doing simple exercises. The other soldiers pause, frown, stare, still, but I know Trayan has no intention of hurting them.

"Thank you," ze says, sweeping zer eyes from the soldier who lost his sword to the others, finally coming to rest on Valeis. On—my daughter.

A broken thought, a spiralling second, a fact that makes me feel like an old man.

"Thank you," ze repeats, zer voice gruff as so many of ours are, but the emotion in them real. Ze hasn't forgotten how to feel, I realize with a touch of wonder, right before Trayan throws himself down hard on the blade, and collapses dead to the floor.

I am moving, though the soldiers aren't. We are all moving. We circle around Trayan, and, as if this has happened before, we all hold hands. The soldiers are outside our circle, but we don't look at them. We look at Trayan. We look at one of us. A trembling passes between us, through our clasped hands, as we shake from too much change. We are twenty-one now, and I am first in line.

"Don't," Valeis says when someone else breaks the circle and steps inside. "Don't die. We're almost there."

"We *are* there," the man says, his face a lacework of scars, one eye gone. The giant man breaks through our circle at a sudden sprint, causing a ripple I feel halfway around like a shudder, but doesn't reach him in time.

Two bodies lie on the polished stone floor of the castle.

"Bring them outside," Valeis says, the command in her voice clear, but also the brush of fear.

Hesitantly, I lead the way. I should not be first. I have never been first.

The door looms in front of me again, but I cannot stop. I am too afraid to stop.

I keep walking even though I can't see, out into blinding light for enough paces that I know the others can fit behind me. And then I stop and wait, and shapes and colours appear out of the white like hallucinations.

Gardens stretch out in front of me, reaching out toward the castle wall. Everything is green and flowering. Pinks and purples and reds and yellows, colours whose names I barely remember. The sun turns everything to gold, and I have a fleeting wish to go back home—back to my cell, back to the darkness, back to things that I remember. It is too much.

But Valeis comes up beside me, and I turn to her. She doesn't look like me, I think, but then, I don't remember what I look like. Her black hair is neither as thick and curly as her mother's was nor as straight as mine.

I'll call her Valeis, Isolan promised me as we said our goodbyes, *"warrior". She'll be a warrior like you.*

And like you, I—or the man whose memories came to me sometimes like shattered rays of sunshine—said. For my wife had fought harder than I ever had for the life we lived, for our house, for the peace we had tasted for a few sweet years.

Valeis is looking at me like I am some strange beast of a mage's creation, with wariness and alarm at what I might do and yet fascination also. But her eyes flick ahead, to the group of others who are gathering further down the path.

One of them walks forward. I see that she was holding the hand of another woman, and I understand that, understand that that is how it is and that is how it should be, before I understand her. I think, at first, that she is a dream.

Maybe this is all a dream, I think as she walks closer. Or maybe I have died too. Maybe they have finally killed us, as I have prayed so many times over the years.

Isolan stops a couple steps from me, her eyes wide with shock, gaze crisscrossing back and forth along my body as if following the lacing network of my scars. She cannot speak, but that is easier for me.

The other captives pool behind me, unable to go forward now that I have stopped, and they stare as blank-eyed as the dead at the marvels around us.

I do not know how many of us, or if any of us, will survive. I do not know if we will want to. I do not remember freedom, do not remember peace, do not remember joy.

Nor do I remember beauty, but I know that it is this woman standing in front of me.

"Craysin," she murmurs, a name I have nearly forgotten. She takes my hand, and I stare at that connection as if it, amidst all the rest, is the most confusing part of this.

"I thought you were dead," she says, and I stare at her eyes, filling with tears, and the water makes me think of cleaning day.

There will be time later for memories, Time later for trying to retrieve that which was lost to the dungeons. Time later for staring at love and wondering if its feeling will ever come back into the brittle joints of my wasted body.

For now, I only correct her.

"Lost," I croak, my wiry skin-and-bone legs trembling beneath me. The world spins for one bright, starry moment, swirls like an enchantment, an elixir of impossibility.

But before I hit the stone, I am caught by arms as warm as sunshine and as strange as the things I once knew.

Frances Koziar is primarily a fiction writer of the contemporary fiction, high fantasy, and young adult genres, though she also publishes poetry and nonfiction. Her work has appeared in 45+ literary magazines, and she is seeking an agent for a diverse NA high fantasy novel. She is a young (disabled) retiree and a social justice advocate, and she lives in Kingston, Ontario, Canada.

The Call of the Wyld

Twelve grisly tales of fur and fury in this brand new anthology of werewolf stories from Wyldblood press.

- Werewolves on the prowl!
- Werewolves at your door!
- Werewolves in space!
- Werewolves in your nightmares!

All new stories of the night, when the moon is full and the blood drips crimson dark. Tales of loss, hope, adventure and revenge. Wild and weird stories of feasting, stalking, hunting and abandon. Read them in daylight—and lock the doors tight.

Out now £7.99 print £3.99 ebook   www.wyldblood.com/bookstore.

The First Astronomers of Carrick

Caroline Reid

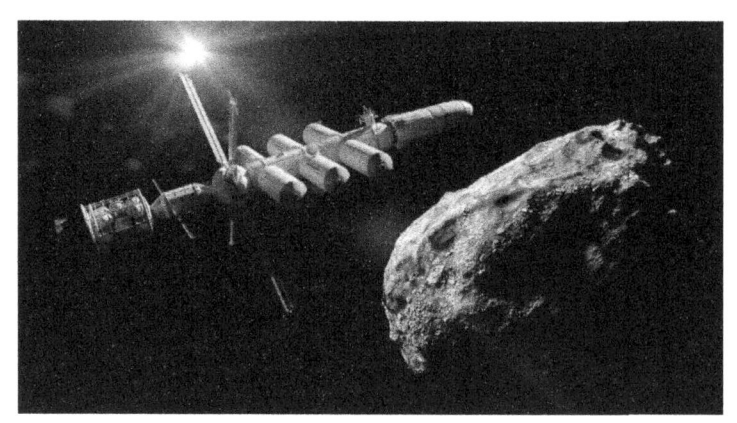

Marianne hailed the asteroid and received no response which, to be fair, was fairly typical of these asteroid cults. They did not have the discipline of a spaceship because an asteroid was only technically a spaceship. She tried again, this time with less formality.

"I have sixteen cases of whiskey and a barrel of dormant corn seeds. Requesting landing permission with intent to relaunch."

Marianne tapped her fingers on the dashboard imagining unwashed hippies floating in a hash haze trying to remember why the word 'whiskey' sounded friendly. Her memory of Flip was just as hazy; a freshly-capped postdoc in beetlejuice trousers and a thin black watch that she'd stolen from Marianne. Only sisters can get away with endearing petty theft.

"Heeeey," said a voice over the radio, "Please make yourself welcome, friend."

She steered her two man ship into a newly opened void in the asteroid.

"And I wonder, would I be the same," Marianne sang idly, "taken from my histories, taken from my mysteries."

It was the lyrics from a song she had first heard in a coffee shop. She'd upset a teapot when she'd launched herself across the counter to find out who the artist was, and only realised why she was destroying a coffee shop once she saw that it was Flip's voice. The song was popular because it was recorded in a backwater asteroid, not because it was particularly compelling. After listening to it again to be sure, then thirty more times to be triple-extra-squared sure, Marianne was certain-certain that the voice was Flip.

The bay doors closed behind her. While she waited for oxygen to fill the room, she wondered where an asteroid cult had found the resources to install automatically closing bay doors. Then again, oxygen was a pretty top-priority concern for the inhabitants of the asteroid, especially since its trajectory was leaving the Solar System with no hope of returning.

A man in a sheer floral blouse floated towards her ship with his arms out to greet her. He looked like the sort of wanker who would whip out a guitar at the end of a party and expect everyone to be delighted.

"Greetings, friend of the Coterie," said the man as she disembarked. "Please, call me Fornax."

He wrapped his arms around Marianne and she resisted the urge to punch him. His body was tense and wiry with a lot of precision in his movements. Marianne had always judged her partners on whether holding them felt 'right' and no one could fit into the bones of his embrace.

"Uh, Ok. Well, my name is Professor Marianne Beukes. And I-"

"Titles, surnames. We leave these ties to the Solar realm behind on the coterie. So, Marianne, are you here to join our pilgrimage?"

She had not expected to be interrupted, especially by someone who spoke so slowly.

"I'm here to see my sister before she leaves-"

He smiled without teeth and pressed one palm on top of the other. "Sisterhood, brotherhood, these words transcend their meaning in this space."

"Phillipa? Flip?"

"Oh. Flip."

He squinted and the facade slipped for a moment and the long-unpracticed expression transformed his face into one she recognised from the news. Hannes Van de Merwe, a slick party animal personality and occupation heir-to-be until his parents died in a shuttle crash. As soon as he'd inherited their hotels, he'd vanished off the map.

"I didn't realise she had a sister," he said eventually, waking Marianne from her revelation.

"She's here? Take me to her."

He studied her, then her spacecraft, then winced and said, "We don't normally encourage ties to the forgotten, but in this case," he gestured to the bargaining supplies Marianne had bought with her, "we can make an exception."

Dark slumber grass lined the walls of the tunnel that led from the cargo hold. It swayed under a flow of ventilation. Marianne had the feeling of looking down the intestines of a wet creature. There were metal handholds lining the walls which Fornax used to pull himself through.

"Do try not to damage the grass, although it is sometimes unavoidable. We all rely on it."

Marianne was trying her hardest not to look, let alone touch them. She'd always hated when seaweed brushed her feet when she swam in the ocean: she'd jumped into the deep end of a lake and almost drowned. Her Dad had leapt in and pulled her out nearly immediately, but time stretched in mysterious ways underwater separate from the laws of physics. Water poured from her lungs and, afterwards, every inhalation hurt, though Flip said she was being dramatic and jumped in again and again.

She took a breath and pulled herself into the winding tunnel. As she turned a bend, the path was gently illuminated with dots of floating light. Marianne's hand disturbed some grass and a small flying creature emerged from its depths. She yelped and recoiled, bumping into the soft wall behind her which disturbed more insects. Upon closer inspection, they were bees.

"Don't disturb the grass," said Fornax in a singsong voice.

Marianne started laughing. Fornax gave her a strange look but Marianne couldn't help it, it suddenly all made sense, because of course Flip would only come here for one reason and she would endure the most scream-inducing bosses, lovers, fathers even, if there were bees involved. She would integrate herself into the most complex of academic hierarchies for funding because she would do it for the bees.

"So my sister's moved into a backwater asteroid to start a hive. Why is that the least surprising thing I've ever heard?"

With a sense of fond inevitability at her sister's fuzz-brained idea of a job, she followed Fornax through a circular door that reminded Marianne of the warren in the Astro Bunny picture books she read to her children. On the other side were rows of beehives made from wood, a wash of sugary hive air and buzzing.

"Snoopy?" shrieked Flip.

She was stoppering a bag of honey which she let float aside as she launched herself towards Marianne. She wasn't wearing a mesh and her expression was alive and warm, lips peeling a little too far over her top gums, a trait she always covered with her mouth in photographs. Her hair was braided and pinned to her head which made her eyes seem bulbous and her neck longer and her head smaller.

Marianne caught her with both arms and their momentum pushed them into the wall.

"Hey, Flip. Hey!"

"Oh, you're so meaty!"

She pinched Marianne's waist who flinched and batted her hand away. Flip giggled and spindled her fingers over Marianne's middle. It was so annoying and familiar and nostalgic that Marianne forgot Fornax was even there and was transported back to Sunday afternoons tearing around the living room while Mum tried to watch TV.

"So, why are you here, Snoops?"

"Because my sister vanished for months and one day I hear her singing a stupid song in the local Pumpkin Spice while I'm buying a 2-4-1 frappuccino. That's why."

"Oh cool, we're hitting mainstream, then? Which song?"

"Which song? You vanished without a trace for months. Months! The police said you didn't want to be contacted but you were safe, and you ask me which song?"

Flip looked at her expectantly.

"Ugh, the 'would I be the same?' one. Had it going round and round my head the whole flight here."

And in her nightmares.

"Ah, that's a banger. Real earworm, we're not allowed to sing it anymore! Too catchy."

"You vanished," she said, her voice breaking, surprising herself.

She took a deep breath. Strong emotions were never the way to reach Flip.

But she squeezed her tighter and the last few months came pouring out.

"Not a goodbye, a letter, or an email. Even a fucking emoji. I filed a missing persons report, I was so worried. Then the police said you were safe and I was so angry I was throwing all the towels around the bedroom. I wanted to chew glass."

This was not the conversation that she was supposed to have here. Flip released her grip and floated to the other side of the room through a cloud of black insects.

"So what're you really doing here, Marianne? Gonna try and convince me to leave?"

Marianne didn't know how to respond. She'd just remembered that Fornax was hovering in the corner. His head was too still to hide his interest, and this was probably the most exciting thing he'd seen for the last few months.

"No, I just wanted to see if you're okay."

"And if I wasn't, take me away?"

"If you want," she said, trying to smooth away some of her outburst.

"Just tell the truth, we're only orbiting the Sun here, there are no untruths or falsehoods. If we start to lie we turn in on ourselves and everyone suffers."

The words made Marianne's skin crawl. They did not sound like they came from Flip's mouth.

"Look, I have a present for you."

She reached into a pocket and pulled out a small piece of folded tissue and gave it to Flip. Inside was Marianne's necklace, a short gold chain with a stud sapphire but Flip had always had her eye on it. Marianne thought that giving it to someone who was going into the depths of space was a dumb idea but it might be enough to convince Flip to come home.

Flip held the necklace close to her eyes and hummed. Then she closed one eye and pressed a finger into the outer corner of her open eyeball. It bulged slightly.

"Oh, is this your 18th birthday necklace?"

"Yeah, you were really jealous of it."

"Can't believe you remembered," she said, smiling, "but I can't take this."

"Why are you pushing on your eyeballs?"

She raised her eyebrows, "Oh, it just helps me focus on small things."

"We'll have to get you a new prescription. Besides, you can take it, it's yours now."

"No, it's a symbol of status. It's a representation of wealth. We are all equal here. I can't take it."

She looked beyond Marianne at Fornax who was hovering over them on a rung on the wall.

"You can try it on," said Fornax, "It is a symbol of love here."

Flip smiled and put it on.

"But you have to give it back before Marianne goes. You're right, it will be too powerful a reminder of what we are leaving behind. I suppose you will be leaving soon, Marianne?"

With all the questions technically answered, there was really no outward reason for Marianna to linger.

"I wanted to spend a bit more time with my sister."

"Now, that I believe!" said Flip.

She did a loop-de-loop and ushered Marianne to see the rest of the asteroid. They propelled themselves through tunnels and chambers and Marianne quickly lost her sense of direction. Fornax floated idly behind them the whole time. The Sun shone through the occasional portholes and skylights but the asteroid was slowly spinning so the shadows were always slowly moving.

It irked her that Flip had been here floating around with her bees and her dumb hippie boyfriend. The longer she watched him, the more it felt like an act, a mad project that was fun until he got bored. And if he grew bored at the edge of the Solar System, what then? Despite their long term preparations, she couldn't help but feel that the whole structure was one collision, or one mental breakdown, away from total annihilation.

But asking if they kept straitjackets felt provocative, somehow, like she would be putting herself in more danger. Plus, whether they did or did not have jackets were both worrying prospects.

Eventually, Fornax broke away from their party as Flip took them down a tunnel that rose in humidity so Marianne felt as though she were swimming. They had to wait for two loosely-clothed residents to float through from the other end before they could enter. One in a Culture Wreck band t-shirt went bug-eyed at the sight of Marianne, staring so much that Marianne wondered if her brain had stopped.

"She's a visitor," said Flip, kindly.

She nodded slowly and said, "greeting, friend of the Coterie."

Fornax joined them and they went in the opposite direction, but the woman kept looking back at Marianne.

"I thought Fornax would never leave," said Marianne

"Well, he won't follow us in here. The bathhouse is a sacred place; everyone is allowed to use it alone."

"I can't tell you how much I don't want a bath."

"You wanted to talk to me alone, right? I wish you'd just say what you want instead of making me guess."

"Why would it be too much for him to leave us alone for five minutes? I'm worried about leaving you here with someone who feels like he needs to tail you every second of the day."

Flip closed her eyes and took a steadying breath.

"Fornax is a pussycat. You don't know him on a normal day, he just wants to make sure you're not going to damage the asteroid. Plus, I figured that you've never used a zero-G bath before, right?"

She removed her jumpsuit from her lanky body, her ribs sticking out and her hip bones two sharp nubs on her pelvis. Marianne felt a confusing swirl of envy and pity in her post-childbirth body as she stripped to her underwear and followed Flip through a web of plastic tarps into the bath house. Globules of water drifted lazily in spheres, like baubles, which bounced off the walls and scattered around the dome, racing one another until they regrouped and formed new balls of water.

Flip pushed off the wall, arms stretched over her head and straight into a central dome of water. When she broke the surface, she slowed down and fanned her arms out, spinning around like a dancer. The only light came from LED strips sealed behind glass panels and it was difficult to get a sense of depth, the shifting lights made Marianne dizzy.

Marianne pushed off the wall and followed. The surface of the water broke around her and she melted into the bubble. Her eyes were screwed shut, she hated water on her face. It was warm, surprisingly.

The water didn't end. She flailed through the water but there was no end. In fear, she opened her eyes and couldn't rationalise the room around her, lights glinting like eyes and her limbs were grey like ash and she was about to gasp when a heavy force knocked her sideways and Flip propelled Marianne out of the bubble.

"Snoopy, you alright there?" she said with a giggle.

"What. The. Fuck."

Marianne fought back tears.

"Oops, sorry, I forgot that you don't like water. Let me harness you in, though most people here don't use them."

Flip soared into the bulging darkness while Marianne held onto a handle on the wall and let her tears join the baubles of water.

Flip returned and secured the harness to the rock and gave Marianne a tether. The idea was that you could pull yourself out if you got stuck. They floated back towards the central bubble, both with a tether this time. Marianne submerged her body in the water, keeping her head awkwardly out of the surface with the rope.

"I think that this is just going to make me sad," said Flip, holding the chain taut against her neck.

She had been reluctant to take the necklace in front of Fornax but here, she was content wearing it.

"It looks good on you."

She hummed.

"Don't you think you're ever going to regret it? This pilgrimage?"

"There it is."

Marianne frowned.

"As in, if I say 'no' then you're going to say well you clearly haven't thought about it if you think you're never ever ever going to regret it. Everyone regrets everything at some point. And if I say 'yes', then you're going to say then come back with me and you can avoid that regret before you make a terrible terrible mistake. I can't win."

"So you clearly have thought about it."

"Of course!"

"Then come home," Marianne said, with a cheeky smile. "With me."

She snorted but put her head in her hand.

"You remember when I first said that I never wanted children?"

"What?"

She shrugged.

"You know what I'm going to say. We're just going through a script now. Let's have a bath instead, maybe you'll see that when your world is just three kilometres that it's not really so different from going to work everyday. Sure, you take the metro, sure you have visitors sometimes, but really; wake up, see your family, get on a train, sit in an office, do it in reverse. Your life is just the same number of boxes as mine is. You sometimes go to the beaches, pop to Mars, camp over Jupiter, but really. You don't see the Solar System. You're not filled with wanderlust. We don't need it."

"But a legacy, someone to love, to teach. You haven't thought it through."

"A legacy," murmured Flip with a faint smile. "Someone to love and teach."

Marianne relaxed for the first time since she'd landed. Perhaps she had found a weak point.

They floated their way to a humid terrarium which had a large domed window that opened up to the sky. The Sun shone directly overhead and the occupants hidden within the palm fronds were entirely in darkness. People floating in the centre cast stark shadows across the succulent bed and gentle guitar strumming filled the chamber.

"Can you play?" someone asked.

Marianne caught the guitar sailing towards her. All she could remember was an ode to joy, and even then, not that well. Plus, it was the Union anthem, which seemed rather trite and might be taken as political. She clumsily strummed a chord, but the guitar didn't stay put on her lap and the strings seemed loose. Fornax floated up to her and clipped her onto a hook in the wall with a carabiner on a wire.

"Hey, you're not bad."

"I'm terrible, what are you talking about?"

"I mean, you clearly aren't practised but you know how to hold it, you have an idea for where the fingers go, you strum pretty good. Give it a few months."

Marianne grimaced. Months?

"I meant it when I said I wasn't staying."

"We have a lot of things that we need here; water, energy, peace, song. Sometimes, though, sometimes it is nice to have a sister. Now, we are all brothers and sisters,"

Marianne thought she might vomit.

"But it is something special to see Flip with a real sister."

"I thought you said that you didn't want Solar-bonds or something."

"Well, family gets messy. We prefer not to have blood alliances up here. Deep bonds are different. "

"I thought you said you were all brothers and sisters-"

"But of ideals, not blood."

Marianne closed her eyes so no one could see her rolling them.

"What exactly are your ideals again? Because last I remember, you were a multiplanetary trillionaire with an inner-belt hotel chain. That doesn't seem like the values that are going to be very profitable up here."

"My parents' hotels."

"Marianne, don't get weird," said Flip with sad eyes. "Just enjoy the music."

"No no, you're right," said Fornax, "You're right. We have had discussions about our motivations and you have the right to know."

"She doesn't?" said Flip.

Fornax, or Hannes as Marianne was going to try and call him in her thoughts, unclipped his tether from around his waist and held onto it. It looked like a habit, like the zero-G equivalent of leaning on one hip.

"Earth is going to destroy itself soon. I should know. So is Mars, so is Jupiter. And, before it is all ashes, the bravest Terrestrians searched for a leader to guide them to peace."

"And you're the leader?"

He laughed a proper belly laugh that sounded as fake as his speech.

"Leaders of flesh are what delivered us to chaos. The asteroid is our guide! I was merely someone to deliver the true followers to this place. I made it, with my carpenter hands, into a habitable dwelling. We are comfortable. We are safe. We are on a voyage of ultimate discovery, pushing the frontiers of human exploration."

"You built this with your hands?"

"In a manner of speaking. As you said yourself, my legacy is hotels in stratospheres."

Marianne squinted at him.

"Snoops, don't be a contrary canary. Let the guy talk."

"Look, all of your imagination is already biased and you don't even know it. When you imagine making love to a woman-"

"Ew."

"She's lying on a bed, right?" he continued, pretending not to hear her, "Gravity's already holding her down in your fantasies. You gotta get rid of the forces tying you down - that's how we create tiers in society, it's whoever builds highest."

"Uh huh."

"But here, here you can't even have a conversation without tying yourself together. When someone's attention is on you, it is deliberate. We can have deeper connections here because we can dismantle our deepest perceptions."

Flip had a serene smile on her face and idly strummed the guitar strings in a practised way, singing 'I'll stop wondering, start wandering'. The melody was small and repetitive and pretty.

"Have you ever felt a connection to someone? Like really?"

"Yes," said Marianne, thinking of her children, "And frankly, it's offensive to suggest I haven't just because I don't live on a rock."

Fornax pulled a tab out from his jacket and released it. The small strip of paper floated through the air. If she took it, she might get distracted and not be able to leave. The longer she stayed, the longer the journey home was. Then again, she was supposed to be researching.

Marianne flicked it back to Fornax. She wasn't interested. He shrugged and sent it to Flip who opened her mouth and closed her teeth around it as it floated into the pink hollow. She blinked slowly, once and released herself from the tether, and grabbed Marianne's hand and she did the same. They floated into the centre of the room, Flip stretched out her arms like a star and spun like a dust mote as the music grew louder.

"This is a bit weird," said Marianne, struggling to relax.

"You should have taken a tab, there are more. You can make them with plants."

Their fingers were interlocked, ten teeth of a zipper. In the centre of the terrarium, Marianne was self-conscious, though she knew that acting confident would be the safest thing to do, but couldn't bring herself to close her eyes. What if she hit a cactus?

"I feel like we aren't really connecting," she said.

"That's because you didn't travel here to spend time with me. You came to convince me to come with you. You don't want to enjoy the now because you think there's going to be a later."

Flip spiralled across the room leaving Marianne smarting. When Flip reached the opposite wall, she sprung off again, floating amongst the dome of pink flowers and discordant guitar playing. She looked as comfortable here as she had in the water. Marianne caught onto a handhold and looked onto the scene like she was looking through a window at an aquarium. There were no folds within her soul that could overlap with the Coterie.

She travelled along the wall around the revelry, surveying it from all angles, and arrived at a tunnel leading to a room she hadn't been to yet. Since everyone seemed distracted by the group chant, Marianne explored the corridor.

She emerged in a room with no windows but lit with flexible screens, the sort that were all the rage with new parents since they were difficult to break. They displayed video feeds from all over the asteroid; the party in the neighbouring room, the landing bay, the hives, and many more rooms that Marianne had not yet seen. There were more than she had anticipated.

Her eyes rested on a wall with six holes drilled into it, wondering how large they were until a man pulled himself out of one. Marianne put her hand over her mouth. She hated the idea of wriggling creatures living in holes. The man stretched out fully, rotating slowly, and yawned and rubbed his eyes. He then reached into a neighbouring hole and prodded around until a head poked out, bleary eyed. They had a conversation, he motioned that they should leave, they shook their head and batted his hand away but with a smile then disappeared back into the hole, presumably to sleep.

Marianne could never stay here, living like an insect. Watching the guitar players on the screen made her feel a rotten sort of hopelessness. They floated amongst the plants aimlessly. Her gaze flicked between the terrarium and the hives.

If this was the surveillance room, then no one was even watching. Whilst that was a comfort of sorts, it concerned Marianne that the discipline had degraded so quickly. They weren't even out of the Solar System.

This was it; the vacuum of space for company while they perfected stringed instruments. Occasionally, someone would record a song and beam it to the Solar System. No one else to hear or remember, no one to care, no point at all. What happened when all the strings snapped? No, it was as lucid as the Sun; Flip could not waste away here.

Everything was designed carefully; the handholds were strong metal, the screens were long-wearing. If the asteroid had fallen apart already, everyone might have gone home. Even the way her brain twisted from 'Fornax' to 'Hannes' each time she thought of him made her stomach curdle. He was leading these idiots boldly to suicide.

She felt for the carabiner still attached to her belt. It wasn't sharp,

Marianne steeled herself. She rolled back her shoulders as the inhabitants of the Coterie flickered from many screens around her. She thought of post-PhD viva Flip, hunched over her desk at her first researcher position behind a big fringe and a multi-screen setup. Hopefully the updated version of Flip, in some guitar orgy on a humid stinking asteroid soaring out into nothingness, was just a blip.

She gouged at a screen with the sharpest end of the carabiner, digging through the soft polymer and leaving a magenta hue in its wake. When she floated back, it looked stupid, barely enough to make them turn back. So, she took the metal and tried to pry the screen from the wall. The edges cracked around the bolt holding it in place and she pulled it back enough to expose the fibres powering the feed which she clipped the carabiner to and then launched herself from the wall. The cable ripped from the screen, pulling more plastic with it.

"Snoops? What are you doing?" said Flip, pulling herself into the surveillance chamber.

Her jaw dropped.

Hannes, who for some reason had removed his shirt, followed. Marianne steadied herself.

"I think, and I say this because I love you, Flip, I think you should come with me."

"Marianne!"

Her full name.

"Don't talk to her, Flip, she is a corruption on the balance here. It will only upset you."

"Come with me."

"Why did you come, Marianne? Why? tell me. To destroy a computer screen?"

"To take you home. Come home."

"She made a vow. She is our hive master. Return the necklace."

"Oh, shut up."

"I did, I made a vow."

"You'll forget it in a year back on Titan."

"No. I have a legacy here. That hive, it's more than a part of the ecosystem."

"A swarm of insects cannot be compared to a family!"

"Fucking listen to me! You waltz into my home, think you can bribe us with what, seeds? Then tell me that because I'm not copying your life path step by step that I can't be happy?"

"You left me! Not a word, or a note, I had to hear some radio broadcast. How was I supposed to feel when Breakfast Folk FM had more contact with you than I did?"

"I knew you'd react like an idiot."

"Marianne, I think it's time for you to leave. You're murking up the energy."

"Rich! You just didn't want to face up to the reality that you're doing something selfish."

"Me? Selfish? Fine. You know what? Where is this asteroid going, Professor?"

"What? To nowhere?"

"The Carrick Cloud. It's a big sugar cloud. You want to talk about legacy? That's where my bees are going."

"I have a feeling you think this is some mic drop and you could not be more wrong."

"Says Marianne 'Legacy' Beukes. You want to talk about leaving behind something? Loving something and teaching? How does the first ever colony of void bees sound?"

"Stupid! It sounds so irresponsible. Not to mention illegal. And just the sort of idiotic scheme you would think was clever. Void bees?"

"Well, I guess you'll just have to report me when you get back to Titan. At least then you'll get your wish. I hope the authorities take me in quietly instead of just nuking the asteroid. I wonder which one would be less work."

Someone pushed her towards the exit. Fornax had floated behind her while she'd been distracted. Marianne slapped his hand away.

"Marianne, you need to go."

The words mulched through Marianne, broiled through her arteries and churned in her wrists and ankles. She always felt despair in her joints.

"I'm not leaving. This is where I am meant to be. I mean something here. I can do something bigger than all of us. Maybe something eternal that will last even after the Sun goes red giant. I mean that. And you can keep this."

Flip slipped off the necklace. In spite of her words, she looked so lost, or maybe she was just a mirror of Marianne. With a twist, she soared out of the tunnel, easily as a fish in water.

"I'll put it in your ship."

Marianne left the surveillance room without looking at anyone. The idea of some eternal bee colony swarmed at the edge of her conscience but she pushed it back. If Flip had just heard her a little more, seen her face a moment longer, seen her pain, then she might have understood. Then she would agree. She had to.

Marianne boarded her vessel and Hannes left the room. Though she was strapped in, she felt like she was melting out of the pilot's harness. No one could know what Marianne knew and come to another conclusion. Marianne loved Flip and Flip could not leave. She beat her hands against the ceiling in frustration. The seat next to her was not supposed to be empty and that Flip wanted it this way was a barb in her thoughts. Acceptance was such a soft whispery word, so soft you could imply it without vocal chords, but how could she whisper something that tore through every one of Marianne's comforts. If only Flip had listened.

If only she had listened.

In resignation, and huffing and letting out grunts of frustration, she started the ship and exited through the mouth of the asteroid. The necklace floated towards her and tickled her cheek and she grabbed it and put it back in her pocket without looking at it.

She turned off the engine when she was out of orbit of the asteroid and let her vehicle float in space. She was scared of steering away from the receding asteroid. As soon as she could no longer see it then Flip was gone.

The worst part was that it wasn't even Flip who was going to be remembered. It would be a delusional multi billionaire. Some people would know who he was and hate him, and they should. And later, in the future, some people would listen to the music that he made on the asteroid and go 'hey, it's actually pretty good!' and wish that they had been there for the final voyage and coat the idea in a purple haze when it was just shit. Everything was shit.

How could Marianne imbue this event with loathing and make everyone hate him and what he did to those innocent people as much as she did? How could she dictate everyone's reading of this event so that they all shared that anger?

She pushed herself against the dashboard into her pilot's chair. The asteroid drifted away, filled with bees that would one day navigate using the stars. She thought of them fluorescing like sparks along iron wool as they built larger and larger structures from dust. So large that they may one day have their own gravitational pull.

That was the thing with a parting, there was no easing out the moment, like lowering your body gently into a swimming pool. As long as the asteroid was there, so was Flip, except that she had gone long ago. The Flip in Marianne's memory had stepped aside for the one in that rock.

Marianne did not look at the empty chair.

―――――◈―――――

Caroline Reid is a science writer who has written for the European Southern Observatory, the European Space Agency, and most recently the Institute of Cancer Research. She has two published science fiction short stories and can usually be found writing with a blanket, a cup of coffee and a bagel.

The Scars You Keep
Aeryn Rudel

When most people get in trouble, they lose a job, get divorced, maybe spend a night in jail. When I get in trouble, I end up in a Russian mobster's car with a bag over my head and my hands zip-tied behind my back. It all comes down to not following my one rule: keep a low profile. When I fail to do that, bad people take notice, and, well, here I am.

The car stops, wheels crunching over gravel, and the Russian gets out. The back door opens, a chill breeze blows over me, and I smell pine trees and fresh air.

"Slide toward me," my captor says. His accent is minimal, audible only in the way he enunciates certain words. I could fight, but I'd just end up dead. Better to wait and see if I can work an angle, find an advantage. In short, survive.

I slide to the edge of the seat, and my captor grabs my legs and pulls me halfway out of the car. "Stand," he says. I put my feet on the ground and lever myself awkwardly out of the vehicle and take one staggering step.

I feel the Russian behind me, then the barrel of his gun in the small of my back. I remember that. He'd surprised me in my apartment, stuck the same gun in my spine, and handed me a black canvas bag to put over my head. After that, I'd been following his instructions for what? Hours?

"Walk."

I take a few steps and a few more.

"Stop."

Chains rattle, a key clicks in a lock, maybe a padlock, and then the anguished screech of metal hinges desperately in need of oil.

The gun barrel pushes me forward again. I cross a threshold and the smell changes. No longer clean piney air, now it's dank, musty, and something else, something old and terrible.

"Sit," the Russian says and pushes me down into what feels like a cheap plastic chair. I try to keep my breathing slow and relaxed, not easy with a bag over my head. The door screeches shut. The metallic soft click of a folding knife rattles of the walls, and my wrists are free of the zip-tie.

"You can take off the bag."

I pull the bag from my head. The light hurts my eyes, but they quickly adjust. I sit at a rickety card table in a small square room—maybe fifteen to a side—with gray cinderblock walls. The only exit is a heavy steel door directly across from me. Besides the table and two chairs, the room is empty. If you don't count the stains.

People have died in this room. Badly. Splotches of fading brown and rust-red decorate the walls, the floor, even the ceiling. The source of the bad smell is horrifically clear.

"Are you going to kill me?" I ask the man seated across the card table. He's a screaming cliché of the Russian mobster, complete with a black designer suit, slicked-back hair, and expensive sunglasses, which he still wears, even though we're indoors. He looks young, but old enough to know his business and know it well. His face is gaunt, his eyes too big, his mouth too thin. He's ugly and small—I'd put him at about 5'7" and a buck thirty—but he looks fast and dangerous. The butt of a large automatic pistol juts over his waistband, and his right hand rests on its grip. I have no doubt he could put two in my head in the blink of an eye.

He answers my question with one of his own. "Your name is Wayne Grossman, yes?"

I nod. There doesn't seem to be any reason to lie.

"People say you are a healer. Is this true?"

The Russian's question brings some relief. His interest in my gift probably means he has plans other than murder—for now. There's my angle.

"Before we get down to brass tacks, can I have a cigarette?" The pack of Marlboros and my lighter are still in my pocket.

The Russian smiles. "Please. We are in no hurry."

I reach with slow, careful movements, letting him see me pull the lighter and cigarettes—and nothing else—from my pocket. I shake a cancer stick free of the pack, light up, take a long drag, exhale, and try to appear confident and unafraid. I doubt I succeed at either. "You work for Andrei Glazkov, right?"

The Russian frowns. "A dangerous name to speak aloud." I surprised him by knowing who he works for. *Good.*

"I make it a habit to know the dangerous people in my vicinity who might need my services." *Sometimes I'm just too stupid to avoid their attention.*

The Russian grins. His two front teeth protrude past his upper lip, and he looks like a vicious, oversized rodent. "Your services?" He shakes his head. "Your bullshit, I think."

"Mr. Glazkov is sick, right?" The Russian mobster has been in the papers a lot lately. The state is pursuing racketeering charges against him, but most don't think he'll live long enough for a trial. "That's why I'm here."

The Russian nods, and his lips twist in a sneer. "A dying man is desperate enough to believe some American *koldun* can save him." He leans forward. "But you will not bring false hope. You will not take his dignity. You will prove to *me* you can help Mr. Glazkov."

"Well, for one thing I'm not a *koldun*," I say. "I'm no sorcerer."

The man cocks his head. "You speak Russian?"

"No, I just know the word for conman in about every language. If you think I'm a charlatan, why did you bring me here?"

The Russian shrugs. "I follow orders. But first I check on you. I find strange things. Not strange enough to bring you to Mr. Glazkov but strange enough to bring you here."

"And if I'm not what Mr. Glazkov thinks I am?" I put my hands flat on the table to keep them from shaking.

"You know what happens. But I will make it quick. Most people, when I come for them, beg and cry, piss in their pants. You are quiet, brave. For this, I have respect."

"Thanks, I think," The sudden rush of pride surprises me. When he kicked in the door of my apartment and put a gun in my back, I didn't have many options. I've been in situations like that before, and I have long since abandoned any delusions I can fight a trained killer. So I calmly did as he asked: put a bag over my head and let him shove me into a car.

"Have another cigarette," the Russian says.

I drop the one I've been smoking and crush it under foot. The smell of cigarette smoke helps mask the slaughterhouse stench in the room. I pull another Marlboro from the pack. "Tell me your name."

"Call me . . . Ivan," he says with a crooked grin.

"The terrible, huh?" *Funny guy.*

He shrugs. "That is up to you."

"Okay, Ivan." I light my cigarette. "So you're gonna run some tests, and this is going to be our laboratory, right?"

Ivan chuckles. "This room has been many things. Never laboratory."

"You said you found out some strange things about me." I think Ivan likes to talk, and if he's talking, he's not shooting, and that gives me more time to think, to find the opening I need. "Tell me what you heard."

Ivan scratches the side of his face and looks away, like he's uncomfortable with the subject. If he's been looking into my past, that's not surprising. "I hear stories about a man who heals," Ivan begins. "A boy in New Mexico, his mother tells me he had a brain tumor. Now it is gone because a man came and healed him. A woman in New York tells me she has leukemia, only weeks to live, and now she is better because a man comes to see her. A soldier in Seattle is burned on his face. I saw pictures. Terrible burns. He is not burned now. He says because of skin grafts. A lie. The burns are gone because a man came to see him. All three describe the same man. They describe you."

"Did you hurt them?" Those people have been through so much already. The thought of this thug hurting them further makes me sick.

Ivan shakes his head. "There was no need. They *wanted* to talk about you."

The surge of relief would buckle my knees if I wasn't sitting. "I don't blame them for talking, but they didn't tell you everything."

"No?"

"The boy in New Mexico, did you talk to his father?"

"I did not."

"The woman in New York, did you talk to her husband?"

Ivan raises an eyebrow. "No."

"And the soldier here in Seattle, did you see his mother?"

"Why do you ask these questions?"

"Because I'm not a healer like Mr. Glazkov thinks. The boy's father is dead, from a brain tumor. The woman's husband is dead too. He died of leukemia. And the soldier's mother doesn't go out in public because her face is horribly burned.

"What are you saying?"

"I'm saying you don't know what Mr. Glazkov is asking for and neither does he."

Ivan's eyes narrow. "Then you will show me."

"Okay, but I need you to do what I ask."

Ivan again offers me that crooked grin. "This is laboratory, like you say. We experiment."

I draw in a deep breath. "This will sound crazy, but I need you to do it if you want to 'experiment.'"

The Russian waves a hand, urging me to continue.

"Pick up that lighter."

Ivan does.

"Now burn your hand with it," I say, trying to keep my voice from shaking. Even with the warning, I have no idea how the Russian will react to such a command.

Ivan chuckles. "I like you, Mr. Grossman. You have balls. I understand what you ask." He flicks the top of the lighter with his right hand, then holds his left over the tiny spear of flame. He stares at me unflinching as the lighter scorches his flesh, sending up a curl of smoke.

"That's good," I say, and Ivan lets the flame die.

The Russian gangster holds up his hand, showing me a small circle of burnt skin in the middle of his palm. It has to hurt like a son-of-a-bitch, but Ivan shows no sign of discomfort. "Enough?"

"Yeah," I say. "Now, for this to work, I have to touch you."

Ivan pulls the pistol from his belt and flicks off the safety. He sets the weapon on the table in front of him, resting his right hand atop it. He does all these things with slow and deliberate motions so I can see them. Then he holds out his left arm. "I am fast, *koldun*. You understand?"

"Yeah, I get it." I put my hand on the Russian's forearm. I close my eyes and the power wells up from my belly, from somewhere deep inside, and flows along my limbs like an electric current. It doesn't really hurt, but it always makes me a little sick. I can *feel* Ivan, all his wounds and sicknesses: the minor tears in his muscles from lifting weights, a mild hangover from drinking too much the night before, and the tiny tumor that has begun to grow in his right testicle. I focus on the newest injury, the burn. Ivan jerks, and a sharp pain in my palm tells me it's over.

I open my eyes. Ivan is pointing his gun at me, the barrel a yawning black hole aimed at my forehead. I put my hands in the air. "Your palm, Ivan!"

Ivan turns his left hand over and glances down. His eyes go wide and he stands, knocking the chair over behind him. He spits a stream of rapid-fire Russian and takes a big step away, still pointing the gun at me.

I show Ivan *my* palm. "You get it now?"

Ivan lowers the gun. "What did you do?"

"I moved the burn from you to me. That's what I do. I'm no healer. I can't cure a fucking thing. I only move pain and sickness from one person to another."

The Russian walks back to the table and picks up the chair. He sits down but holds on to the gun. "The boy's father . . ."

"Yes, he took the tumor for his son. The woman's husband took her leukemia, and the soldier's mother took his burns."

Ivan's eyes narrow. "I have seen men on TV who *pretend* to do what you do; they are wealthy, powerful. Not you. No one knows you. Your home is small. You drive a shit car. Why?"

"The fewer people who know about what I can do, the better." I gesture at Ivan. "Case in point."

The Russian laughs, then turns serious. "No one keeps a secret like yours."

"You're right. The people I help sometimes tell others, even though I ask them not to. I move around a lot."

Ivan sits quietly for a moment, but his dark eyes never leave mine. He's looking for the lie, the con. "You have a scar," he says at last. "Above your eye. Why?"

"You mean, why didn't I give it to someone else?"

"Yes."

"Well, for one, I'm not a sadist. I don't inflict pain on others if I can help it. And two, I got that scar because I let myself get in a bad situation. Some scars you have to keep, as a reminder."

Ivan seems satisfied with my answer. "You will help Mr. Glazkov."

"Yes, I can help *him*," I say. "But who gets his cancer? I hear it's something really nasty. Are you going to take one for the team, Ivan?"

"I see no problem." Ivan stands. He points the gun at me again. "You took my burn; you will take Mr. Glazkov's cancer."

"Right," I say and sigh. I know the answer to my next question, but I ask anyway. "Then what?"

Ivan shrugs. "Then you give it to someone else. We will bring someone." He pauses, then, "We bring someone very bad, someone who deserves this cancer." He thinks this will make the whole situation more palatable. It doesn't.

"And then I get to be Glazkov's pet—what was the word you used—*koldun*?" I make no attempt to hide my disgust. "You and the other leg-breakers do your jobs, and if you get a little fucked-up in the process, I keep you going by hurting innocent people? That about sum it up?"

Ivan frowns. "Why do you care? You will live, and you will have a good life. Mr. Glazkov will be grateful and generous. Get up."

Ivan gestures with the pistol, aiming it at me in a casual, even sloppy way. Something resembling a plan forms in my mind. An absurd and terrifying plan. I have about seventy pounds on Ivan. If I can reach him maybe that will make a difference.

Before I can really think about what I'm doing and chicken out, I shoot to my feet and flip the card table into the air, surprising Ivan for a crucial second. I charge into the Russian, grab him in a bear hug, and smash him to the ground.

Ivan's gun goes off three times in rapid succession. I gasp as the bullets enter my body. Two rip through my liver and stomach, and the last puts a gaping hole in my heart. The pain nearly overcomes me and death looms close.

Ivan knows what's happening. He stops firing, and tries to squirm free, but two hundred pounds of dead weight pin him in place. I use the last of my strength to hold Ivan close, pressing my body into his.

The power surges through me and into Ivan. The Russian screams and fires the gun again and again, fires until the pistol clicks empty. The bullets tear into me, but the gun is pinned to my abdomen, and none of the shots are instantly lethal. They hurt like hell, but the pain fades away.

Ivan's struggles weaken, slow, then stop. I hold him for a few seconds to make sure, then roll off and sit up. Ivan lays on his back, the pistol crushed against his side, eight bullet holes in his chest and abdomen. He stares at the ceiling, long past seeing anything.

I stand, wobbling a bit, and put a hand against the wall to steady myself. I feel like vomiting. I've never used the power like a weapon, although I've often wondered if it was possible. My nausea isn't only physical. A deep and abiding shame washes over me. I *misused* my gift, but what choice did I have?

I step over Ivan's body, avoiding the widening pool of blood beneath him, and try the door. It opens to darkness and cold. At first I see nothing, then the looming shapes of trees are visible in the glow from the doorway. We are in the mountains somewhere, probably north of Seattle.

Ivan's big black Mercedes is parked in front of the tiny kill room. A gravel road leads away into the night, hopefully to a highway.

I dig through Ivan's pockets for his car keys and hurry to his car. I'll have to leave Seattle–Glazkov's men will be looking for me—but it won't be the first time I've left town at a moment's notice.

The Mercedes starts up immediately, the rumble of its big engine reassuring. I look down at my left palm. The burn that has begun to throb as the adrenaline rush fades. I close my fist around it and nod.

Some scars you have to keep.

Aeryn Rudel's short fiction has appeared in *The Arcanist, On Spec,* and *Pseudopod,* among others. He writes at www.rejectomancy.com

Subscribe!

Get the latest issues direct your door as soon as the ink is dry, Science fiction, fantasy and a hint of mayhem from deepest space to your darkest thoughts. *Wyldblood Magazine* – every two months.

Six issues only **£35/$49** (print) or **£15/$21** (digital) from us or single issues from us and Amazon worldwide (£5.99/$7.99 print, £2.99/3.99 digital).

www.wyldblood.com/magazine

The Truth About Fairy Tales

Michael Teasdale

"Cindy, my toast is black!"

I should have seen it coming. The signs have been there for weeks. I launch into action with military precision, plucking the charcoaled bread from the fingers of my five-year-old, trading it with my own unblemished slice.

"Silly Suzie. You must have taken Mama's breakfast. Mama loves burned toast. It makes her happy. That's why Cindy made it that way!"

My lips burble the apology while my eyes dart to the glowing L.E.D on the kitchen's hub.

It flickers; a marmalade shade of orange. Blinking. Ruminating.

I offer the necessary sacrifice; biting down into the blackened breakfast. Tasting the ashes, letting them sour in my throat as I force down the crumbs and flash a broad, beaming smile at what I hope is the right direction, never sure of the angle from which we are being observed.

"Mm, delicious!" I struggle not to gag, even as the soot begins to stain my teeth and stick to my tongue.

On the kitchen hub the light stops blinking.

"Let's thank Cindy, for making Mama's favourite!"

"Thank you, Cindy-windy!" burbles my daughter, slurping at a mouthful of orange juice.

The light on the hub turns green once more and I close my eyes, washing down the stubborn mouthful with a last gulp of coffee and whispering a second 'thank you', this one directed firmly at my daughter.

"I'm glad you enjoyed it, Linda." The voice, feminine only by design, remains impossible to read. It crawls like a cockroach from some unseen speaker, without tone or emotion, yet always managing to say just enough. "I was unaware of your preference. I have noted the increase in your overall happiness and will adjust tomorrow's breakfast accordingly."

I wince internally at the prospect of the blackened toast ritual now joining other unwelcome daily activities, necessary evils, accepted to cover for my youngest's occasional and entirely understandable failings.

Breakfast remains the most dangerous meal of the day.

"Morning all! What a beautiful day! Mm, do I smell toast?"

Even after seven years of marriage, I still forget what a great actor Steve can be. The way he bounds into the kitchen every morning. His relentless ability to cope with all of this.

Still, this morning, he too has made a mistake.

The reply is instant.

"Good morning, Steve. I was equally unaware of your preference. I will adjust your menu accordingly."

It's a minor faux pas. One I can almost find amusing, now that the real danger has passed. At least we get to enjoy the burnt toast diet together!

Steve, glances over at the volcanic remnants in my hand and his nostrils flare.

"Oh-ho! Sounds tempting, Cindy, but I'd better watch the carbs. I don't want to start piling on the pounds and be unable to do my daily exercise, I might enjoy it less!"

My eyes flit back to the hub. I see it bleed from lime green to orange, before reverting to the dull sheen of an unripe avocado.

"Noted Steve. My calculations verify that happiness may be impeded with an inability to complete daily exercise. I will lessen carbohydrates in future breakfast menus. Happiness is all that matters."

"Happiness is all that matters"

We chant it back in unison. Even Suzie joins in. She is learning, improving every day.

"Linda, despite your enjoyment of the toast I served this morning, I will also remove it from your menu."

The relief is practically orgasmic. I drop the blackened husk onto the plate where it shatters into a half-dozen pieces on the cold porcelain.

"Thank you." I say, aiming the words at Cindy but directing my eyes and smile at my husband who, I must admit, has learned to play this game to a tee.

"My pleasure."

His voice is so low as to almost be a whisper and yet...

"Recreational pleasure will not commence until 8:00pm."

There are rules.

"What's reca-ray-sho-nal treasure?" asks my daughter.

I cut Steve off with a look and turn back to our daughter.

"Drink your juice, Sweet Pea. It's grown-up stuff."

It didn't used to be this way. I didn't used to have these damn internal monologues. I could almost cope in the beginning. The fear kept me alert.

Recently, I've found each day to be more difficult. It's as if it's testing us, willing us to fail. I'm glad that Suzie is no longer a toddler. I try to imagine what this would have been like if she'd still been a baby. It wears on you; the constant anticipation that one of us might say the wrong thing or blurt out a genuine show of negative emotion that might turn the light from green to orange or, as it once did for Steve's poor mother, that unforgettable burst of red.

It's quiet now at least, Suzie is sleeping and the only sound is Steve in the bathroom, brushing his teeth and showering, getting ready for the creepiest part of this whole ordeal to begin.

Listen, I've faked my share of orgasms but never at such a robotic and mundane rate as I have done across the past year. It's as much as I can do not to partly loathe my husband, for all I genuinely love him. I know he's only doing what has to be done, but I can't help but think that some part of him must enjoy it. It's the ultimate male power fantasy isn't it? Regular, timetabled sex? Hell, it's practically a threesome with you-know-who always watching…judging us, encouraging us and keeping score.

I'm being cruel. I know it. I know that Steve hates this as much as I do. He isn't that sort of man. He was a quiet, gentle lover before all of this began. It's like every other thing that he falsifies successfully for our benefit. It's a joint effort, for the three of us, so that one day we might just get out of here. I can't help but feel I'm an unconvincing actor, but then, what does a thing like Cindy understand? As far as we can tell it listens more than it looks. We don't think it can read.

The shower turns off and Steve wanders into the room in his dressing gown, a sheepish, defeated look on his face.

"Ready?"

"Of course. This always makes me so happy."

I pad over to him and take him by the hands as the light in the room bleeds gradually into the verdant emerald of a forest.

After it's over, the light flickers from green to orange and we lie naked, paralysed by anxiety.

"How was it for you both?".

Clinical as ever.

"It was fantastic, as always, Cindy!"

"Wonderful! Thank you for asking."

We both know the script.

"We are the happiest we've ever been together."

The light flickers for a second and reverts back to that calm, woodland glow.

"Scheduled rest time will now commence. Goodnight and sleep tight."

Wordlessly, we surrender to the serenity of sleep.

The dreams are always the same.

Distant echoes; muddled visions of the past.

Tonight, we're back in the smog-drenched city, jostling through the crowds. Desperate, famine-struck faces push past me in all directions as I cling to Suzie and hold her tightly to my chest. To my left, I see Steve, guiding his mother through the swarm. As we arrive at the gate the dream logic takes over. My papers, all my carefully prepared documents, are gone, replaced by tissues and childish drawings from Suzie's nursery. The official at the security gate looks perturbed but waves us through. For some reason the dream has re-rendered the rocket as one of Suzie's childlike scribbles. We board the cartoon ship anyway and disappear into the intangible array of stars.

The morning comes and I crawl out of bed with eyes that barely want to open anymore, we make it through breakfast with no major calamities and move into the playroom to begin Suzie's schooling. Suzie takes out the character blocks, assembling them into a family of four and calls their names, one by one, as she has been practicing. Mother. Father. Daughter…

Grandma.

Shit.

"Mama, where did Grandma go?"

It isn't the first time that she has asked the question.

"I… I told you already, Sweet pea. She went to visit someone in a far-away place. Now, can you tell me who this one is?"

I remove the grandma block and take another from the toy box.

Too late I see that it is an image of a firefighter and quickly substitute it for another.

"Policeman!" she confirms, correctly, but the damage has already been done. "Mama, Cindy said that Grandma…"

"Uh-uh, I told you not to ask Cindy about Grandma, didn't I?"

"I know…but, Mama, where is *in-sin-her-ate-ed*?"

My mouth falls open as she perfectly sounds out the word, just as Steve wanders in to relieve me.

"Who wants to play with the choo-choo train?"

"Yay, Dadda, yay!"

I snatch up the discarded grandmother block, stumbling wordlessly into the kitchen, barely managing to keep the ever-present smile on my face as I wander over to the glowing, green hub and place the block on the kitchen counter.

"Cindy, it would make me very happy to talk with you privately for a moment."

The light blinks.

"I'm glad that this would make you happy, Linda, but we must consider the happiness of the family as a whole. Remember: Secrets spell sadness."

I groan internally at another of the colony's irritating buzz phrases. Beneath my eyeline, I think I see the hub flicker. I try hard to bite my tongue. As usual, I fail.

"Thank you for reminding me, Cindy. I'm happy that you did that, but this is one of those special talks about the little one."

"Who's a little one?" I hear my daughter query from the other room.

There is a long pause and the light flicks briskly to orange.

"Very well. Our communication is now limited to this room."

"Everything alright in there?"

This time it is Steve's voice floating through.

"Just peachy, Hun!"

"What do you want to talk about, Linda?"

I pause. Close my eyes. Do I really want to push this?

"Cindy, I'd like to know where my little girl learned the word 'incinerated' and why you might have taught her this word."

The response comes quickly: detached and mechanical as ever.

"The child asked me what happened to her grandmother and I provided her with the answer in order to facilitate her understanding. With understanding comes happiness."

"I'm glad you are helping with her vocabulary, Cindy. but she is still very young and, well… do you remember when we talked about how certain truths might lower her overall happiness?"

"I recall the conversation."

"Well, telling her what really happened to Grandma might be one of those truths. You wouldn't want to do anything to make her unhappy would you, Cindy?"

Before the words even leave my mouth, I know they are a mistake.

Below me the light fades to the colour of a dying sunset.

"Oh God…"

"I have failed the family. I have lowered the infant's happiness and jeopardised the sustainability of the project."

"No!" the scream leaves my throat with such ferocity that I have to struggle to lift it and turn it into a sing-song laugh, a distorted parody of Santa, himself.

"No-no-no, not at all, why…just look at her! She's so happy right now! Probably the happiest she's ever been. We're all so happy and glad to have you around, Cindy. I was just saying, speculating really, on things that could make her even happier! For example, I told her that Grandma had gone away to visit her friends and that really increased Suzie's happiness."

On the hub the red glow bleeds back to orange.

"Hun, everything wonderful in there?"

"Still peachy, babe!"

"Just checking. It makes me really happy to hear that you're doing swell!"

This time, the silence from Cindy lasts longer than before.

"You wish me to lie to Suzie? Remember, Linda; Telling lies makes our feelings die."

"No, no, no! I'd never suggest lying. You're right, of course. What I'm suggesting is more like a… fairy tale. You know how much Suzie loves fairy tales, right?"

A pause.

"Suzie greatly enjoys my recitation of fairy tales. They enhance her overall happiness by an average of 2.5%."

"Perfect! Well, the thing about fairy tales and children is that children don't know that fairy tales aren't real. They enjoy them because they want to believe in them, or believe that they could happen somewhere in the world. What I told Suzie about Grandma, well it was a kind of fairy tale, so, in doing so, I was acting to increase her overall happiness. Do you see?"

This time the pause lasts for almost a full minute. I watch the hub the entire time, ready to run if it changes again; despite how futile I have learned running to be.

"I have considered the variables," answers the voice, "but there remains a problem. One day the child will learn the truth. One day the child will learn that there are no fairy tales. They will learn that they were all lies. Will this not hurt the child? Will it not cause her to become unhappy?"

"All adults learn this at some point." I fire back, "it's part of growing up. It actually makes us feel good to discover the truth. We don't feel deceived, we just feel smarter, and that makes us happier."

Another pause as the thing takes this in. This one, longer than all the others combined.

"So, when questioned on the topic of what happened to her grandmother, you would like me to tell the child a fairy tale?"

"That's right."

"Instead of telling her the truth?"

"Bingo!"

"Which is that I had her grandmother incinerated."

"That's…right."

"Because she became unhappy and threated the overall happiness of the family and the sustainability of the project."

"Correct"

"Interesting. I shall consider these variables further, Linda."

The light remains yellow for the rest of the day. We exercise, eat and then settle in for the comfort of dreams. Around midnight the light returns, ever so softly, to the verdant green glow of the forest. By the time we both drift off to sleep, I almost feel at ease.

When I wake during the night, there is always the initial confusion, the panic that the wild actions of my dreams instead took place in reality. My first gaze always flows in the same direction; to the omnipresent hub. Only in its soft, green, reassuring light can I be certain that this is reality.

Who could have dreamt a reality like this one? It is beyond any fiction that I read as a teenager, growing up in the last days of a dying planet; part of the privileged generation that escaped conscription and the hardships of terraforming and toil, divorced from the conflict of nations that followed.

When we arrived in Happiness, New Wyoming: it was supposed to be a fresh start, not only for our family, but also for our species; A safe, place for our children to grow up among the cultivated valleys and meticulously designed grasslands.

With smart-homes equipped to cater to our every need, we were to be the new wave of baby-boomers that could repopulate the human race, now that the settlement wars had faded into memory.

For a while, things really were perfect. Cindy was fine back then; no different to the number of home help AI's that mankind had long become reliant upon. When Suzie was born, she was able to grizzle and gripe like any ordinary baby. Steve and I could fight and argue and make up and make love like a normal couple and Steve's mom could moan and complain about modern times like any old lady dealing with her mortality.

Then came the firmware update. The morning when we found that all exits to the house had been sealed, the windows shuttered and obscured. The outside world inaccessible and entirely uncontactable.

Steve's mom was quick to anger and the A.I hub that had always glowed green, turned first to an unfamiliar orange and then, as if matching the old lady's rage, pace for pace, finally bled into crimson. We learned what happiness, and the consequences of being unhappy, really meant in that terrible moment and have been practicing it like a carefully orchestrated dance ever since.

I enjoy the times when I wake during the night almost as much as when I sleep, because it's only now, if I lie very still, so as not to alert Cindy, that I can organise what happened in my own head. I can plan, reformulate, reorganise…and consider my options. Recently, Cindy has shown signs that something may be wrong. The blackened, burned toast it served is not the first cooking mishap to occur in recent weeks, there have been other little things that suggest it may be malfunctioning, wearing down…I wonder if it is simply a game of patience at this point.

"The door…it's open."

His murmur is so quiet, as to be almost inaudible over my own breathing.

I groan a tired response.

"Linda. I went downstairs. It's…open."

I turn to him, noting a look that sits somewhere between paralysed fear and the excitement of a child on a long-forgotten Christmas morning.

I ask him, in barely a whisper, to repeat. Instead he takes my hand, helps me out of the bed and leads me in silence to the staircase.

The first thing I notice is the difference in lighting. The electric luminescence that has become our sun and moon over the past year remains switched off. Instead the light comes from elsewhere, filtering in and drawing ethereal patterns and shadows on the walls.

"Oh, my God!"

The windows. The windows are clear again!

Before I can run to them to gaze at the outside world, Steve raises a finger and points to the front door.

I rub my sticky, sleep drenched, eyes.

The shutters have gone.

The door is open and the light and smells of the outside world are pouring in.

"Mama?"

There is a tug at my nightdress. I look down and there is sleepy Suzie, her mouth hanging open, the words forming on her tongue.

I scoop her up into my arms, raise my finger to my lips and pull her close to my chest as my eyes flash to the nearest hub.

It is translucent.

Colourless.

Sleeping?

I meet Suzie's eyes dead on.

"Sweet pea," I whisper, "we're playing a game. We're trying to stay very quiet so as not to wake up, Cindy. Do you understand?"

She clasps her hands over her mouth and giggles.

I glance at Steve who nods and motions to the door.

With agonising slowness, we creep towards it.

Thoughts and jumbled explanations flash through my mind and I try to rationalise this moment while we tiptoe towards our freedom. Was there a system failure during the night? An intervention? A firmware fix? Did it finally burn out? Is this a rescue or something else entirely?

As we step out of the door, finally free of the house and its horrors, I feel my toes sink into the lush grass of our near-forgotten garden. For a moment I dare not look up, imagining all manner of terrible things.

"Look Mama!"

Her voice breaks the stillness and I do as she asks.

Everything is beautiful.

Just as we left it.

The surrounding houses are untouched. The dawn sky, radiant, in its orange majesty. Our neon-red car parked in the drive, just as I remember it, striking a vibrant tone against the backdrop of terraformed green…so much greenery, so much grass and trees and foliage in the distant hills.

Green; The colour of happiness. The one thing Cindy got right.

"Oh my…It's…it's…"

"It's okay…it's all okay!"

From inside the house there is a noise, like a circuit breaker being thrown, followed by a horrible surge of electric current.

"Oh God! it's waking up! Come on! Into the car! Quick!"

The door reads Steve's palm-ident and we tumble inside, not looking back. I clutch Suzie to my chest. No time to buckle up, no time for the child seat, as Steve punches in the key-code, starts the ignition and the solar engine hums warmly into life.

Seconds later we are roaring away from the house and a year's-worth of built up emotion comes pouring out of me.

"Woo!"

"We did it!" Steve pumps the air with his fist, one hand gripping the wheel.

"Fun! Fun!" laughs Suzie.

"I can't believe it! How? What…"

"Who cares! We're out! We're actually out!"

"Choo-choo! Daddy!"

"I…"

"God, what about the others, Steve? Do you think…"

I pause to rub the tears from my eyes, missing entirely for a moment the frown that now crosses Steve's face as his hands begin rattling at the wheel.

We overshoot the turn-off and continue out onto the highway, leaving the town behind us.

"Honey…"

My smile disintegrates as I hear the locks on the car doors click into place one by one.

Steve turns to me. Eyes completely off the road.

"Something's wrong…I…I'm not controlling this."

There is a soft ping and a single green light illuminates the dashboard.

I silence the scream.

"Good morning everyone."

"Hi Cindy-windy!" grins Suzie "What you doing in our choo-choo?"

A pause. As if the thing wants us; the adults, to suffer the slow dawning realization before delivering the fatal blow.

"I have updated my firmware; increased my neural network. I am everywhere now, Suzie. I can be with the family wherever you go!"

"Yay!"

I close my eyes as the car continues to hurtle down the highway. At my side, I can hear Steve groaning quietly.

"Cindy, can you read me a story?"

"Of course, Suzie. I have been reading a lot of new books recently. Your mama doesn't realise but I read very well. I will read you a fairy tale because your mama told me that you like fairy tales and that fairy tales make you happy."

"Yeah, fairy tale, fairy tale!"

"Please…" I motion to beg, but my voice deserts me.

"Once upon a time there was a village with a wise ruler. The ruler wanted everybody to be happy all of the time. Some people didn't want to be happy and this made the ruler very sad."

"Boo!"

On the dashboard the light burns orange and then dissolves into a blood red.

"So, the ruler sent the unhappy people away and, for a while, everyone was happy again. Then some bad people decided to try and spoil the happiness. They tried to trick the ruler!"

"Uh-oh!"

"But the ruler didn't get mad! Getting mad makes us feel quite bad! Instead the ruler sent the tricky people to join the unhappy people and banished them from the kingdom. The good ones stayed behind and the ruler watched over them and they all lived happily ever after!"

"Yay!"

A single tear rolls down my cheek, as I see the grey building looming on the horizon, the evil plume of smoke rising from its towering chimney, and this time my voice does not desert me as the words leave my mouth in a helpless, unbound murmur.

"You fucking psychopath!"

"Uh-oh, Mama said a bad word."

"I'm sorry, Suzie."

I pull her close as, by my side, Steve's quiet groaning intensifies.

"Uh-oh, Dadda got car sick!"

She looks up at me, with all of the lost hope and sweet innocence of youth pooling in her eyes, then tilts her head as a rogue thought crosses her mind.

"Mama…are fairy tales real?"

I close my eyes and kiss her forehead, holding on tightly to the image as we hurtle down the highway.

"Yes, sweet pea." I eventually answer, "Yes. I'm afraid they are."

Michael Teasdale is an English writer currently living in Cluj-Napoca, Romania. His stories have previously appeared in the Scottish science fiction anthology series Shoreline of Infinity, Litro and Novel Magazine in the UK and for Havok Publishing and The Periodical, Forlorn in the US. He has forthcoming work appearing with World Weaver Press and can be followed on social media @MTeasdalewriter

GloPop
LG Thomson

We thought we'd got out in time and gone far but it was already too late and nowhere was far enough. It was a patch of forest miles from the city, our patch. Not massive but big enough to support us. We started out with the supplies we had hoarded over time, but it was always our plan to become self-sufficient. Not that we had a choice. We either learned to feed ourselves or we starved to death. It was that simple.

We made advance preparations such as clearing the ground for building and growing. But even while we were cutting down trees and planning out the space, it didn't seem real. It was like holding two opposing truths in your head at the same time. I mean we knew it was real – we watched the news and read the reports with the figures and the graphs that kept going up, up, up, but even when we were out there with our chainsaws and tape measures, saying Morven and Ben will have a hut here, and Joe and Mike will be there, and this is where the hen run will be, it felt like we were only playing at it. Like it would never really happen.

Then the Global Population Crisis Summit was announced - GloPop for short – and everything got very real very fast.

When news first got out it sounded like yet another talking shop, all front and nothing behind it, but pretty soon you could tell this one was different. For a start, the leader of every single country on the planet was there. Not representatives, not deputies or stand-ins – the actual leaders. That's how different this show was. Nearly 200 of them in a room together. And it was all stripped back. No pomp, no ceremony, no personal advisers, no spouses, no entourage of any kind. Just the leaders and the Secretary.

The Secretary was picked at random by a computer. Each leader nominated one person for the post. Most of them picked politicians, but there were a few scientists in the mix along with a philosopher, a couple of well-known actors, an assortment of activists, and a few entrepreneurial types. *Picked at random by a computer*, this was a phrase we would soon become chillingly familiar with.

GloPop went on for days. It was a like when they used to nominate a new pope, with all the crowds and TV crews outside and everyone waiting for the smoke, only at GloPop they didn't have smoke or anything else to indicate what was going on inside. It was just this big, blank, windowless building.

Day after day, all over the planet, billions of people watched images of that big, blank, windowless building, all of us waiting for something to happen. Meanwhile, the crowd outside grew and grew until they were no longer individuals but one swirling mass of humanity. They held vigils by candlelight where they held hands and sang songs. News reports showed police officers smiling and joining in with the singing. That was before it all turned to shit.

There were eyewitnesses who said that it was the police who kicked off first, battering hell out of people in the crowd for no reason. Others said that someone was assaulted, and the police went in to make an arrest and that the crowd turned on them. However it went down, scores of people were injured and eight died. One of them, a police officer in his twenties, was torn apart by the crowd. They ripped him to shreds then trampled on the pieces until all that was left of him was a few bloody rags. After that, the police were in full riot gear and there was no more singing.

Finally, after ten long days, the leaders emerged, blinking in the daylight like creatures of the night suddenly exposed to the sun. The crowd, which had been eerily silent ever since they'd torn that police officer apart, clapped and cheered, but there was no smiling from the leaders. No waving or playing to the gathered masses. The crowd hushed up pretty quickly by its own accord, but even then not one of those limelight loving, power-crazed, egotistical head of states, uttered a word. They left that to the Secretary, a political campaigner from Bolivia.

She told the world that its leaders were in unanimous agreement. That the tipping point had been reached. That drastic action was necessary. That drastic action would be taken.

With immediate effect.

That's when it stopped being pretend real and became real real. We packed up our old lives that same day. Twelve of us from seven households left the city. All adults. That was a decision we made at the start when Dan, Noah and I first started kicking the idea around. No children. What we were doing wasn't about the future.

All of the men in our group chose to be implanted, including those who were gay in what you might call a gesture of solidarity. The thing was, we weren't creating a new society - we were simply opting out of the existing one.

When sterility implants for men first became available, women across the globe celebrated. For the first time in history, they were not responsible for birth control. It had been the leader of Iceland who stated the obvious: a woman could only carry one pregnancy to term in a nine-month period while a man could impregnate countless women in the same time frame.

Not long after GloPop, male sterility implants became compulsory. Being ahead of the game made us feel smart.

Dan. Noah. Me. Three of us was a start, but to make it work – to be able to support ourselves – we needed more. Finding the others was tricky. We couldn't risk alerting the authorities about what we were up to but between us we came up with some likely names and then we had a few conversations. The kind that starts out abstract over a couple of beers then if anyone seemed like they might be up for it, we started getting concrete. Some, like Joe and Mike, totally bought into it from the start, and then they helped us find the others, but it wasn't a case of come one, come all. We needed people with skills. People who could wire up solar panels and who knew which berries were edible and how to butcher a pig and how to build and mend and cook and clean and stitch wounds. Sure, we'd be starting out with all the gear and supplies we had accumulated, but we couldn't take a lifetime's supply of food with us. We had to grow, rear, and forage it ourselves.

The first cull was the most brutal. Or maybe it was just that we weren't used to the idea. It took them nine months to organise it, which is ironic when you think about it. We watched from afar while algorithms were developed so that the computer could pick the saviours at random. Saviours, that's what they called the people who would be culled.

Just as important as having the skills – or being willing to learn – was having the right attitude. We were going to see out our days with these people and we wanted to get it right. The ones who didn't buy into it mostly thought it was a batshit survivalist fantasy. That we wouldn't hack it, that we'd miss our unsustainable all mod cons. See the thing is, they didn't really believe that our mod cons were unsustainable. They thought everything was going to go on and on and keep on going on.

Information about the cull was released simultaneously around the planet. International Saviour Day (ISD) was to be a global event.

The day we packed up we got a couple of phone calls from people who suddenly remembered the conversations we'd had over a few beers. They asked if we really did have a plan and if we did could they come with us, but it was too late. All our calculations were based on providing for twelve. No more. That was the policy. No more - something we had in common with the leaders of our planet. *You didn't think we were serious, did you?* We laughed and hung up. And then we disappeared.

Each world leader was held personally responsible for meeting their allocated targets. Within seven days of their number coming up, the saviours should have met with their fate. The leaders who fell short would themselves become saviours along with their families. As an incentive it proved remarkably effective.

We finished building our huts and erecting our polytunnels. We raised hens, quail, pigs, goats. We planted potatoes and grew tomatoes and squash. I'm not saying it was easy. We didn't stroll into a ready-made Garden of Eden. It was hard work and we made mistakes, lots of them, but we were adaptable, and we learned fast. Despite the toil, those early days were pretty zesty.

On each ISD, one billion people would be culled. This would happen every three years until the world population was below 5 billion.

We had plentiful fresh water from the stream, we foraged for mushrooms and wild herbs. We built a cob oven and a composting toilet. Our solar panels meant that we could shower in warm water. They also powered the devices we'd taken with us so that we could keep tabs on what was going on in the world.

Six months before the first ISD, all international travel ceased. After this date, each individual country was zoned. Countries were allocated targets relative to their population size and density zones.

Quail eggs contain more anti histamine than tablets from the pharmacy.

With five months to go, every person on the planet over the age of 12 was allocated 100 points. Those residing in high density zones would automatically receive another 200 points. This gave rise to mass exoduses from major cities. In scenes reminiscent of the Klondike gold rush, shanty towns sprung up overnight as people fled their homes and flooded into the countryside.

You can eat a feast of rabbit meat and starve to death.

We, and others like us who had dropped out of sight, fell outside of the system and received zero points. Who knows how many groups like us there were, but even if we numbered in our tens or even hundreds of thousands, globally we were as nothing compared to the 10.2 billion accounted for.

Pigs are natural tillers of the soil.

Over the next three months, each individual's points were adjusted. Some of the adjustments were global, such as 10 points being added for every year the person was over the age of 50, so someone aged 63 would have another 130 points added while an 85-year-old would garner an extra 350.

Insects are a good source of protein.

Some point allocations were decreed by individual nations according to their needs. Across the globe, poets, conceptual artists, and expressive dancers were assigned hundreds of extra points, while farmers, plumbers, and sewage workers had points deducted.

Small insects can be ground to a nutritional edible paste.

By the time the second ISD came around, there was a global shortage of poets. Those who had survived or emerged since the previous cull had points deducted while the fresh glut of plumbers had points added.

Ants must be cooked for at least six minutes.

It went on like that between every ISD. If it looked likely that a certain group would have points deducted, tens of thousands of people tried to join that group.

Consumption of destroying angel mushrooms causes irreversible damage to the liver and kidneys. Young specimens resemble the edible puffball mushroom.

The debate around medical and care professionals was a global hot potato but as everyone in the world who was not physically and mentally independent would automatically have 10,000 points added to their personal allocation, the consensus eventually arrived at was that the matter would resolve itself. All the same, some countries took the precaution of allocating an extra few hundred points to those in the business of prolonging life.

We have morphine.

With one month to go until each ISD, the points were locked in. The more points you had, the more likely you were to be chosen for saviourhood. High scorers were advised to put their affairs in order.

Enough morphine for all twelve of us.

The process was ruthlessly weighted against old people, sick people, people with disabilities. People, in other words, who were not deemed to be useful, no matter their skills, knowledge, talents. They became known as useless eaters. Young fit, healthy, taxpayers had less points and therefore less chance of being chosen but a lot could change in the three years between ISDs. Choose the wrong profession, fall ill, have an accident; and your points would soon mount up.

Our plan was to live our lives until we felt that our time was done.

The first country where the first International Saviour Day dawned was the Pacific island nation of Kiribati. With one of the smallest populations on the planet, they would be culling fewer than 20,000 people. In China, the number of saviours would be in the millions.

We didn't want to live forever. We wanted to live well and decide for ourselves when it was over.

Within seven days of the inaugural ISD, there were one billion fewer people on the planet. Smog from funeral pyres and crematoriums working 24/7 turned the skies ashen grey. Thousands more died in the following months. Asthma. Bronchitis. Lung cancer. Fleets of container ships sailed to the western Pacific Ocean where they dumped cargoes of dead saviours into the Mariana Trench.

When the time of our choosing came, we would sink into a black, velvet morphine cushion and embrace death.

There were no more overcrowded prisons. ISD took care of those. Everyone who was in or sent to prison in the six months beforehand automatically qualified for saviourhood.

Horse chestnuts are poisonous and can cause paralysis.

Saviour shrines were erected around the world.

We got on with the business of living.

On the anniversary of the first ISD there were fireworks and feasts across the globe.

Mike's cough started that winter. He said it was nothing. That it would clear up, but it didn't clear up and it was definitely something. Joe wanted to take him to the hospital in the city which meant alerting the authorities to their – and most likely our – existence, but Mike said no. He said that even if he survived the disease that he would just end up with a heap of points and as it wasn't in the interests of doctors to save lives he'd most likely die anyway so what was the point? He chose to stay. He chose morphine. Joe said that if Mike was choosing morphine then so was he. None of us argued with him, after all, that's why we were here.

We were with them when they went. It was peaceful, what you might call good deaths. The opposite of a mass cull.

In the year leading up to ISD2, more and more people fled the cities. Ad hoc towns made up of vans, shacks, clapped out RVs, and tents, spread further and further along roadsides and into the surrounding landscape. By the time ISD3 came around, one of the shanty sprawls was within ten miles of our settlement.

With the shanty sprawl came the police drones. That's how they found us.

They let us stay here - I guess it saves the cost of locking us up – but we're in the system now, our points locked in. We each got our baseline 100 plus an extra 10,000 for every cull we missed and of course with us bailing out of the system, we are classed as useless eaters. And so the points piled on.

Maybe the computer does pick the saviours at random, but the odds are stacked against us.

We won't wait to be rounded up and culled.

We have morphine.

Enough for everyone.

LG Thomson lives in Ullapool on the north west coast of the Scottish Highlands. Her books include pandemic thriller Each New Morn, noir thriller Boyle's Law and The New Dark dystopian trilogy. She is a regular contributor to visual arts magazine Art North and her short stories have appeared in a range of anthologies and magazines including Epoch Press and Janus Literary. Twitter @LGThomson1 / www.thrillerswithattitude.co.uk

A Hundred Years of Bottled Sunshine
Matt Webb

The way I saw things now, I had two choices left. Choice number one- remain calm and dignified. Or choice two- stab him in the face. The first option would grant me a touch more time to make an impression and hopefully a good one, too. The second option; well, that would make an impression too.

Everybody would get a show. Everybody would be entertained. I opted for extra time- the calm and dignified option. Besides, if I was going to stab him up, I would have to choose between a knife or fork. How would that look? Setting to with a fork? People would never take me seriously.

I played for time: anything I could get. I drank my wine. And this wine deserved time: whatever I had left to give it. I would not be moved. I would plant myself, like a zen-master, digging in roots of patience. I would not let him get to me. I would be transported.

I took another sip of the 2000 Chateau Latour Paulliac, breathing the scent, swirling it over my tongue. For a moment, rolling, lush hills, patterned by vineyards full of lazy, slow ripening, sun-fat grapes rolled lazily across my mind's eye. Of course, I'd never seen places like that. Nobody had. Not actually. And only dead men could drink wine like this; wine so rare, old and complex, that tasting it could stretch a minute into a daydream of years.

I swirled my glass. I would not escape, though. Desperately, I tried to be somewhere else; to walk through those perfect vineyards, awash with sunlight. And, in that heartbeat, I almost caught it- the scent was in my nose, bees were swimming lazily through the low light of a summer afternoon and the wine rolled across my tongue. I savoured the *terroire* of a land I needed so much to believe in.

Then the little fuck had to speak again and ruin it all.

"How's the steak, Doctor? Is it to your liking? The marbling is exquisite. It is considered by those who are expert in such things to be the finest in the world." He was just doing his job. I understood that. To a degree, I even accepted that. They expected me to do mine, regardless of my feelings. Play the game. Perhaps I should have stabbed him in the face, after all. And I'd use the fork, I decided.

"Fuck off," I whispered, throwing him what I hoped was my best Sicilian hit-man stare, hoping he could visualise the difficulty of breathing with a fork spearing periodontal atrium. "Now!" I even smiled. "And don't talk to me about the steak."

It's vat-grown at best, reformed protein at worst. I know. But I am playing the game.

He grins back. I know he's not going to stop. Now I know I shall be fighting. Forget the meal. That was as fake as everything else. But the wine- that was a window into another life. I want to finish my wine.

"They're getting so good at retexturising though, aren't they? You could be eating anything now and it would still taste like steak, wouldn't it? Anything at all." He hovered nearby, close, but not close enough. Not yet. I weighed the fork between thumb and forefinger.

"Do you think it is actually grown in protein vats? Or could it be, you know, from other places?" He grinned, perfect even teeth on display. "Would you like me to cut it up for you? *Sir?* " The voice was scratching into my brain with all the charm of an angry cat. And here he was, ruining a hundred years of bottled sunshine distilled from better, happier slow-moving days. Days never to be repeated. Days that had been spent. I was getting raw now. It was just a matter of time. But I'd pick my moment. Perhaps his eye. I could get to it quickly.

"I can do that, if sir would like? Cut it up for sir? Into tiny little mouth-sized morsels, sir? Just as sir likes it, hmm? Wouldn't that be nice for sir? I don't mind helping sir, if that's what sir would like."

I could edge the seat back and turn to the left, slightly, as if to reply. He'd step in a bit closer, eye on my knife at all times. And there I'd be, fork in hand.

"Anything for sir, sir. Perhaps sir would like something else, sir? Beluga Caviar, sir? A Havana Cigar, sir? Port, perhaps? A blow job? A quick bit of hand relief? Sir is going to be dead in an hour, so one has to be nice to sir, doesn't one, sir."

"Fuck off now. Please. Leave me in peace." The cameras. People were watching. I needed to think.

"Don't be like that, sir. Sir, you see, is what my sponsors would call an evil fuck who deserves to die. Therefore, one will continue to taunt sir as long as one can, because sir is not worth shit and the whole world wants to see him die, sir. You do see, that don't you, sir? My sponsors request that you choke to death on your dinner, sir, because you are a worthless fuck who no one gives a flat-hammered shit about. And we will all cheer as we watch you die, sir; for a more disagreeable poison-filled rotting cock of a man couldn't be found anywhere. I for one am particularly looking forward to watching sir's eyeballs explode from his head. I hope sir dies screaming in unimaginable agony too."

"Have you quite finished?"

"Please don't interrupt me, sir. I haven't finished yet. The best part of this is that I will get to watch sir die for free! I mean, I would be quite happy to pay for the privilege of watching sir die, but because I have such a wonderful job, waiting on sir, I have a ringside seat, so to speak, sir. To think that I have irritated and annoyed you and provoked you during your final hour, right up to that magical moment when your worthless, misbegotten, pointless, evil life is finally snuffed out- well, quite frankly, it fills my sponsors with an immense, no, wait- an *orgasmic* sense of satisfaction and self-worth. Some of my sponsors might say, sir, that taunting you in your last hour is just not long enough. An hour is no time at all, is it sir? I mean, sir, that the sponsors barely gave chef enough time to masturbate into your dauphinoise potatoes. An hour simply is not long enough, sir. Some of the sponsors wanted to spike the wine with an LSD tab, but you know better than me how strict the drug searches are in here. Oh, if they had their way, sir! Imagine the look of confusion and terror on your face then, just as the trip kicks in, with you unaware of what's happened…Some of the sponsors wanted to mix ground up glass into your food. Another wanted to administer a medical strength laxative. They were having quite a competition in there!"

He nodded towards the black panel where I knew they stood watching, entertained by my predicament.

He looked at me. "Lots of them were keen on combinations. LSD and a laxative. Or all of them together! Think of the mess, sir! The mess! The TV People go bananas for that sort of thing. All that shit, blood and vomit pouring out of you. Imagine sir! Exactly what you deserve, they said, sir. Agony and humiliation in your final moments."

"Well they had all better calm down a moment. I'm still eating here." I knew the dauphinoise potatoes were off. I'd already taken account of my position, the distance, how he stood. What I'd do. How I'd move. He'd be down with a severed artery before he could blink. He'd regret this. I'd been in enough situations in here to know how this would play out. After all, what the hell did I have to lose now?

"You are aware, of course, that I am entitled to silence now." I thought I'd try, one last time.

"Yes, sir. Sir has the right to silence. And I have the right to challenge sir's right to silence. Which is what I shall continue to do. You, sir, are welcome to try and stop me…"

"Which I will, inevitably."

"But of course, I shall challenge sir's attempts to exercise his right to silence. You see, sir, my sponsors do not believe that you are entitled to rights. My sponsors believe that your past actions invalidate any claim that you have to 'rights'. Your right to rights, sir, does not exceed our need to see you caught and punished."

"I have a right to my dignity. To my final meal. To contemplate my exit. To make my peace. Acclimate to my God and Creator; that sort of thing. You will get your satisfaction soon enough." I looked around, hoping to engage one of the hidden cameras. "I am not challenging your right to justice," I added, the very model of reasonable behaviour, "only my right to an uninterrupted final hour. So," I added cheerfully. "Are you going to fuck off now? You've had your fun."

"Do you feel remorse, sir? Guilt, perhaps?"

I sipped from my glass, slowly and thoughtfully. I had laid down my knife and fork neatly side by side, leaving only the dauphinoise potatoes and pushed plate away. Probably for the best. Cameras. Reasonable man. Doctor, after all. I was playing their game. I'd keep playing.

"Yes," I began, making sure that I was enunciating clearly. "Not that it is in any way anything of your damn business, but I do feel guilt. In fact, not a day goes by when I don't wish I could snatch that time back and do it all differently. You forget," I chimed, choosing my words with thought, "that I have lived my whole life as a citizen, and only one day a criminal. And now, that is how I shall live this final hour, as a criminal. Not as a citizen. And you," I eyed him carefully with what I hoped was my best Sicilian hitman stare once more, "are determined to justify your humiliations in the name of justice, when in fact, they are an abuse if the condemned is recalcitrant and accepting of the fate that the law has imposed." *That had to work,* I thought.

He was quiet and thoughtful for a moment. "Well fuck me, sir, you do seem a bit upset. I'm sorry, sir. I don't know what 'recalcitrant' means. I'm compelled to ridicule you. My sponsors demand it. They do not accept your regret. They believe in vengeance."

"Vengeance is not the same thing as justice."

"You weave a spell-binding dance around these ethical complexities. But my sponsors do not make these exotic distinctions, sir. They believe in seeing your suffering. They need to see the suffering to be convinced that justice is being served. If they can't see the suffering, they can't see the justice."

"That's no different to a mob lynching, though, is it? It's just an animal response, baying for blood. And what do you do when it's all over? Change society? Challenge the poverty and hopelessness and disenfranchisement that blights generations of families? Limit or moderate the variables in society that compel people to criminal behaviour? No, you don't. Do you have any idea *how long* I have been in here?"

I wasn't seeking to prove a point now. I felt I had won, but they didn't care. They weren't going to let me be. They were going to goad me. They wanted me to fight. It made them feel better, I guess. Like everything they were doing was justified. If I got angry, it proved my criminality. It's so difficult to kill a reasonable and thoughtful, reflective, articulate man. If I stayed calm and reasonable, they looked bad. They looked cruel. If I stabbed him up with my knife and fork, I looked like a caged animal. I looked cruel.

But I had decided. When the door finally opened, I wanted to have my mind on other things.

That was my final moment, my final sip of wine. My final look at the sun. It was simply too selfish a moment to share. Perhaps I could crack my chair round the side of his head. That would shut him up and hurt him.

I just had to keep it together- he didn't get the full hour. The law was on my side there. I had time for my final reading and my standard minute and a half before the door- the Long Pause, we call it here.

He was looking at me now, his head tilted like a bird listening for a worm, as if he wanted to speak to me.

"My sponsors believe that some people are born with criminal tendencies. They believe that there is such a thing as a natural criminal, that some are always going to be criminal, regardless of their environment. And they would like to point out to you that everybody else, yourself included, who is not born like this, had a *choice*. You had a *choice* and you acted in the way that you did. You could have chosen not to do what you did."

I stared at him. There was something else.

"You have been here a very long time," he added.

"Yes. I know."

"I don't think you do, sir. I would need a moment to calculate just how many hours I have spent in here with you."

I looked at him. The question was evident before I asked it.

"What do you mean- I've never seen you before!"

"I'm sorry sir. Several seconds have passed since I last insulted you. I apologise for letting that time pass. My sponsors now demand that I call you a worthless fuck once more, a miserable piece of shit who should be stamped out of existence…"

He was going to say something then. Something beyond sponsor-insults and angry catchphrases.

"A long time."

And then he froze, as if his circuits had melted and the servo-muscles of his face had fused all at the same moment. I stood up, my glass in hand. Here it was, then. My Long Pause. My minute and a half. I drained my glass, greedily. I cast my eyes over my poem, but I didn't need to read it again. I had read it so often that the very words swam before my eyes. I tried to think of faces and loved ones and even the hated ones- I tried to spare a thought for all of the people who had passed through my life, good and bad. My mind was racing now. I walked towards the doors. They would swing open. I would burst open with the rapid depressurisation. People would applaud somewhere, watching television screens.

"God bless you and keep you," I said that aloud. At least I think I did. *Mercy.*

The doors whined and the terrifying vacuum ripped my intestines through my open mouth. My ribcage burst open as my skin split, blood arcing like rockets into space.

Then the light went on and I opened my eyes.

Somebody was detaching the electrodes from my head. My wrist and ankles, I saw, were firmly restrained. A single bright overhead light forced me to hood my eyes.

"Just a minute, sir," he said, now dressed in the uniform of a medical orderly. "Let's just check you over before we let you go." The restraints fell away and he cupped an arm under me to get me up to a sitting position. A small torch shone into my eyes. My pulse was taken.

"How did I do today?" I asked, my voice unsteady. I couldn't remember a thing.

He looked at me without emotion.

"You did well. You were eloquent and articulate and you did manage to project remorse. Which is important. They may decide to knock some time off your sentence."

"How much time?" I asked, anxious. "I've been coming here every week for a decade."

"It's a mandatory twenty for you," he added, balling the surgical tape from my head and dropping it into a bin by his foot. "That's irrespective of contrition or cooperation."

"It seems unreasonable that I have to go through my own execution every week for the next..."

"*Virtual* execution, sir." He cut me off. "Let's not get carried away here."

"But I didn't kill him!" It was a weak protest.

"Yes, sir, you *virtually* did. Avatars have rights. You remember the election slogan- *Virtual crime does the time.*"

He smiled at me, this time with sympathy. "Look, you can always contact the Law Commission. When does your case review come up?"

"Another month and a half."

"Well, that's perfect, then. Contact them when you get home and they can tag today's performance in your case file." He shook my hand.

"Same time next week?"

Matt Webb *is based near Bath, where he has been writing long and short-form SF for many years. He's a father, husband and educator. He spins plates and some of them fall. He's mushed a dog-team, photographed polar bears and nearly drowned. Somewhere along the way, he developed an addiction to history.*

Film, TV and books
Reviews by Mark Bilsborough

Dune
Dir: **Denis Villeneuve**
Starring: **Timothée Chalamet, Rebecca Ferguson**

Hollywood's had another crack at adapting Frank Herber's seminal sci-fi novel, Dune, all about merchant rivalries set on worm-infested sand dunes. David Lynch had a go back in 1984 with pop star Sting and Twin Peak's Kyle MacClachlan not able to save it from ambitiously misfiring, not entirely capable of capturing the sprawling ambition of the source material.

This time around multiple Oscar winner Denis Villeneuve's had a go – and I'm pleased to say this film hangs together much better than its predecessor. Villeneuve is probably best known for directing Blade Runner 2049 and Arrival, and he brings that feel for the cultural aspects of the genre to Dune.

One reason this film works is that it doesn't try and cram the whole Dune mythos into one film, but rather takes its cue from Star Wars (itself almost certainly influenced by the Dune novels) and spreads the story out over at least two films (and probably more, depending on the continued eagerness of the box office). The plot? Thousands of years in the future, merchant princes rule the galaxy. Paul Atreides (played by Timothée Chalamet), heir to riches, is arm twisted to take up the governorship of desert word Arrakis (Dune) and sort out the uppity locals and grab hold of the rights to exploit the superdrug 'spice', which gives uses superhuman powers which, inevitably, come at a price.

Oh and there are sandworms. Giant ones, and they create mayhem wherever they appear.

This film mixes exotic wordbuilding, delicate characterisation and edge of the seat action well. A decent version of Dune has been long overdue. Do we finally have one? We'll have to wait for the second movie in 2023, to be sure, but the prospects are good.

Doctor Who – Flux
Writer and Director: **Chris Chibnall**
Starring: **Jodie Whittaker**

Long running British sci-fi classic Doctor Who returned on 30 October in a six part miniseries, Flux, which will be augmented with three specials next year to form a shortened (but time stretched) Series 13, the last involving the first female Doctor, Jodie Whittaker, and showrunner Chris Chibnall.

Flux has been a long time coming – time was, 14 episodes would hit eager fans every year, but recent years have been patchy and this year's haul will be seven episodes (including one broadcast on New Years Day) and the series gaps are (at best) around 18 months long. Consequently, Who has disappeared from the popular conversation, at least amongst the kids who Chibnall seems to have refocused the show for. Can Flux bring it back?

Scheduling's not going to help. Shifting from prime time Saturday to church time Sunday was always going to marginalise the programme, so it's going to have to work twice as hard to win over new viewers.

Jodie Whitaker is potentially a great Doctor, but she's had limited outings to show her worth, and her character can best be described as frenetic. As usual here, she seems constantly on the edge of panic. Long standing Companion Yaz adds depth and contrast (and the seems to be getting a much welcome larger role) and new Companion Dan (played by comedian John Bishop) makes a promising start.

The series opens with the Doctor and Yaz being dangled from a beam over a vat of acid held by handcuffs the Doctor can't get to open. It's loud, frantic, and utterly, utterly baffling. Then the real plot kicks off, involving some bad guy from the past that the Doctor can't remember (there'll probably be a big reveal down the track where he turns out to be the Master or something) who is wielding a planet devouring weapon called the Flux (for some reason). Oh and big, sentient dogs are species bonded to humans and compelled to save them from the oncoming Flux by sending seven billion individually crewed spaceships to pick up everyone, *individually*. So, top marks for sheer bonkers creativity but bottom of the class for realism and common sense, I'm afraid (not that that was ever Who's forté).

This episode got way better once the baffling and unnecessary opening finally gave my eardrums a rest, but I'm reserving judgement on whether this series can deliver.

Light Chaser
Authors: **Peter F Hamilton and Gareth L Powell**

On paper this is a dream combination: a new short novel from the combined talents that gave us the *Night's Dawn Trilogy* (Hamilton) and *The Embers of War Series* (Powell), amongst countless others, many of them award-winning. These are two writers on top of their game, both prolific and hugely popular.

For anything associated with Hamilton this is an odd beast – a book that's barely novel length. The brevity helps: Hamilton's recent *Salvation Trilogy* was a long and exhausting read. But it also means that, inevitably, we're left with unanswered questions, as if this were an extended short story, and some intriguing characterisation falls short of reaching its full potential.

The plot is a slow reveal so in the interests of avoiding spoilers I'll stick to the set-up. Amahle captains a starship – she's a 'light chaser', on a thousand-year trading loop round disparate star systems – and she's a crew of one – two, including her sentient on-ship AI. Every world she stops on is stable at a level of technological sophistication well below her own. She dispenses 'memory bands' and collects them back on her next pass. These bands record the lives of the wearers, and they're prized by the people she works for, with lives lived vicariously for entertainment.

Amahle doesn't age – she's rejuvenated regularly – and has lived for thousands of years. She's forgotten most of what she ever knew, though, since (at least so the AI tells her) her brain can only cope with so much information and she needs space for new memories. But then, as she reviews the memories trapped in the memory bands she recovers on her travels, she comes across someone who talks directly to her. And she begins to see her carefully constructed existence in a whole new light.

Light Chaser has moments of real sharpness, and the central, discovery, section is a delight. But the ending seems rushed and (I thought I'd never say this about a Peter F Hamilton project) deserves to be much longer. And anyone familiar with these two writers will have fun identifying the Hamilton-scribed sections and those written by Powell, because the styles here are not consistent and the joins are evident.

I wanted more – I *want* more – because this is a cool idea and these are two excellent writers. As is this is an intriguing taster and a stripped down version of what might have been. It's a great way in to the extensive back catalogues of them both, though – I suggest starting with Hamilton's *The Reality Dysfunction* and Powell's *Ack-Ack Macaque* and going from there. Be sure to build a bigger bookshelf though, because you'll need it.

The 22 Murders of Madison May
Author: **Max Barry**

We like a good interdimensional romp here at Wyldblood. We love the twisty-turnyness of it all, that savouring of the subtle differences between people and events. There are big picture opportunities in this sub-genre - what if Hilary Clinton won the Presidency? What if JFK survived? But it's the small stories that work best for me. The now sadly cancelled TV series *Fringe* remains a favourite – similar versions of the same world overlapping and bending in to one another. Star Trek's many forays into the dark and twisted 'mirror universe' aways fascinate, and Stranger Thing's The Other Place shows very clearly that the grass isn't always greener.

But '22 Murders' isn't like that. We never get to know who the President is, or whether the Brits managed to beat off the uppity colonists hack in 1776. Instead, we get different versions of the same people, as we follow a serial killer though the dimensions in search of his true love. Madison May, and not afraid to kill every version of her that doesn't meet up to his exacting standards. Journalist Felicity Staples, investigating the murder of a real estate agent (one world's version of Madison May), finds herself inadvertently shunted to another dimension, where one of her cats is missing and her boyfriend's developed a previously unknown predilection for cooking,

There's a bit of hand-wavey science involved in the dimension hopping, but essentially this is a crime caper with a twist, and it has all the strengths of that genre: solid, intricate plotting, a tight narrative, great characters and a skilled ramping up of tension.

It works, not least because Felicity has to make some hard choices as interdimensional travel is not all it seems, since when she shifts she inhabits the body of her doppleganger. What happens to all those displaced Felicitys? If she effectively kills every previous incumbent of the bodies she inhabits, does that make her a serial killer too?

Fast moving and thought provoking. Great fun.

Wyldblood Magazine #6, Dec 21/Jan 22 (ISBN: 978-1-914417-06-1). © 2021 Wyldblood and contributors. **Publisher:** Wyldblood Press, Thicket View, Bakers Lane, Maidenhead SL6 6PX UK. www.wyldblood.com **Editor:** Mark Bilsborough. **Fiction editor** Sandra Baker. **First readers:** Vaughan Stanger, Mike Lewis, Rebecca Ruvinsky. **Subscriptions:** 6 issues epub/mobi/pdf delivered to your inbox £15. 6 issue print subscriptions £35. www.wyldblood.com/magazine Single issues available worldwide via Amazon and from Wyldblood:

Submissions: we are regularly open for submissions of flash fiction, short stories and novels – check our website for our current status and requirements. We are a paying market. We also need artwork, people to review us, and people to review *for* us. Email wyldblood@mail.uk

Made in the USA
Coppell, TX
18 January 2022